Homicide at

Harmony Bed & Breakfast

A Travel Writer Mystery

Rebecca R. Pappas

This book is dedicated to my family and friends. Thank you for your love and support.

ACKNOWLEDGMENTS

First and foremost, I would like to thank the Lord. Without You none of this would be possible. To all of my family and friends. You have given me years of love, support, and encouragement as I strived to make my dream come true, thank you. I am truly blessed to have all of you in my life. To my amazing KRJS writing group, thank you for hours of reading, edits, and laughter.

CHAPTER 1

Harmonyville, Georgia was exactly what the brochure had promised.

Old attached brick buildings formed a circle around a community park where a dozen or so people strolled across the buzzed grass. The surrounding buildings housed boutique shops and cafes with small outdoor tables. Vibrant orange, yellow and purple blooms in large flower pots flanked doorways and street lamps. Wooden benches tucked under window awnings and throughout the park gave rest to grey-haired ladies. The town was idyllic.

I sat at the stop light and watched a couple of teenage girls struggle to hang a banner from two petite trees: *Welcome to the 10th Annual Harmonyville Fall Festival.* Vendor booths were positioned along the far side of the lawn and a few people had begun to set up chairs and picnic areas in front of the gazebo where the band was doing a sound check. I turned off my radio and rolled down my windows to listen to the ensemble play snippets of jazz, intermingled with happy shrieks from children on the playground. I took a couple of photos for my travel article with my cell phone before the light turned green.

After traveling a half a mile, I came to a small raised bridge that led to the residential area where a sign warned drivers to "Watch for Children." The two lane street was lined with Victorian and Craftsman style homes. I had just passed the fourth house on the left when I saw the black and white sign hanging from two whitewashed wooden poles: Harmony Bed & Breakfast.

I turned into the driveway and looked for a place to park, only to see all four spaces were filled. I pulled back on to the road and spent the next five minutes parallel parking my car in front of the Victorian. A nip of cool air brushed across my face when I got out of the car. I looked down the road in the direction I had just come from and decided I was close enough to walk downtown; my sedan could stay where it was for the next three days.

Trees shaded portions of the yard and rays of sunlight poked through the somewhat bare branches giving the house a feeling of warmth. I dug in my purse for my new phone, a thirtieth birthday present to myself. I took several pictures from different angles making sure at least two photos highlighted the white picket fence surrounding the front yard.

When my mini photo shoot was complete, I pulled my black suitcase out of the trunk, slung my computer bag over my shoulder, and headed up the sidewalk. Just before entering the gate I stopped short, closed my eyes and took a deep breath inhaling the scent of wood burning from a fireplace, nearby. As I started up the walkway crisp red, brown, and yellow leaves crunched under my feet bringing me back to my youth and Octobers in Connecticut when my dad would rake leaves into piles just so I could jump in them.

I climbed the front steps and stopped to admire the wraparound front porch decorated with pumpkins, bales of hay, and a child-size scarecrow.

Several sets of white rocking chairs with small tables in between them ran the span of the porch. In the curve of the veranda a young couple, who looked to be in their early twenties, was seated. They sported matching spider tattoos that crawled up their necks and piercings in their lips, nose, and ears. His short brown hair was spiked with red dye on the tips, and her long black hair had patches of purple stripes.

They looked my way, smiled, and waved. I returned the gesture then walked toward the door, pausing in mid stride when I heard the young girl laugh so hard she snorted. It reminded me of my best friend, Olivia, and I wished she were here.

I was reaching for the doorknob when the door abruptly swung open. I stepped backed, sucked in a pocket of air, and threw my hand over my heart. "You startled me," I said, and smiled.

The man stood in the entry, his green eyes digging into my face. He clenched his thin lips together so tight they turned white. I was about to ask him if he was okay, but before I could get the words out he walked over the threshold, slamming the door behind him. He grumbled something I couldn't make out as he passed by me, knocking into my shoulder. I watched in amazement at his rudeness as he stomped down the stairs, threw the gate open, and started down the sidewalk.

The young couple were looking in my direction. Their sympathetic smiles assured me I wasn't the first guest to encounter this man. I shrugged off the man's discourtesy and stepped inside the B & B.

I let my laptop continue to hang from my shoulder and set my suitcase down in the foyer, next to the staircase. My eyes were drawn to the black and white photos of men with thin mustaches and women with buns that sat on top of their heads that hung on the wall leading upstairs. I assumed they were the family I read about that built the home in the 1800s. I wondered how they would feel about strangers coming and going on a weekly, if not daily, basis.

I turned my attention to the exquisite mahogany desk with gold brushed handles located against the far wall of the foyer. A stack of brochures and notepads were neatly positioned by a cup of pens. The only other things in the room that I could see represented the twenty–first century were sitting on that desk: a lamp, a laptop computer, a printer, and credit card machine.

A faded pale blue and cream color Oriental rug complimented the dark tones of the room and covered most of the hardwood floor. An antique claw foot table with matching mirror decorated the wall opposite the stairs. The open doorway to my right exposed a cherry wood credenza and dining room table that could easily seat ten. To my left was the living room. A grey haired woman with glasses perched on the end of her nose sat on the rust colored antique sofa rhythmically working two knitting needles. Two large cats kept her company. The Maine Coon was curled up in a nearby chair and the black and white tuxedo cat was stretched out against her thigh.

I was looking down the hall, past the living room and in the direction of the kitchen, when the smell of Ralph Lauren's Polo pulled me back to the foyer. I turned around to see where the heavenly scent was coming from and saw the most attractive man I had ever seen in person making his way up the stairs. He looked like a runway model: tall, broad shoulders, and brushed back dark brown hair with a few loose strands hanging over his forehead. I stared at him unapologetically. Could this town get any better?

"Hi," he said, looking back at me as he climbed the steps. He displayed a perfect set of teeth and a pair of eyes so blue they could have come straight out of the waters of the Caribbean.

"Oh...um...hi," I said. I could feel the heat rise in my cheeks.

"Hello, you must be Kate Westbrook!" A woman's energetic, high pitch voice filled the room.

Startled, I twisted in her direction. "Hello, yes," I said, and then took a quick peek over my shoulder at the stairs. He was gone.

"Oh, honey, don't I know it. He got in this morning. I don't know if the girls in Harmonyville are going to know what to do when they see him. We don't grow 'em like that around here. I'm Cora, by the way, I run the B & B. Welcome to Harmony Bed & Breakfast." The petite host spread her arms wide then brought her hands together with a loud clap. Cora couldn't have been more than five feet tall, seven inches shorter than me. She wore her sandy blonde hair in a shoulder length bob which complimented her radiant face that showed little signs of aging.

A younger version of Cora, with long surfer girl blonde hair, entered the room from the hall. "This is my daughter, Mindy," Cora said.

The pretty young woman nodded and gave a quick smirk then turned around on the tips of her red heels and headed to the desk. Mindy may have looked like her mother but she most certainly didn't have the same disposition. Cora didn't give off the air of arrogance Mindy possessed.

"She helps me in the evenings and on weekends sometimes. We get so busy this time of year with the festivals and all," Cora said. She took my credit card and walked over to where Mindy was printing out a form for me to sign.

There was still a hint of Polo in the air and I couldn't help but take in a quick breath. I glanced up the stairs with the hope I would see him, but only his cologne lingered.

"Okay, everything looks good," Cora said. She held up a key chain in the shape of a music note with two keys dangling from the ring. "The gold key is for the front door and dead bolt. We *never* leave the doors open. The cats stay inside and I don't want to take a chance of them getting out." She smiled and nodded but her eyes told me just how serious she was about keeping them in the house.

Cora continued her speech. "The door is dead bolted at 9 p.m., however you're welcome to come and go as you please. The silver key is for your room which is up the stairs, last door on the left, number four. Breakfast is served every morning at eight." She walked across the hall to where the old lady sat, still knitting. "This is the living room where we serve hors d' oeuvre's every evening at five o'clock. The two furry ones curled up asleep are Watson and Goose. I named Goose. He's the black and white one lying next to Mrs. Brandon. My daughter named the other cat. She's more of a Watson kind of girl, if you know what I mean."

I wasn't sure I did know what she meant, but I nodded in agreement.

"Oh, Kate, before I forget," Cora said and strode past me to my suitcase. "We serve dinner on Sunday nights and since you're not checking out until Monday we would love for you to join us."

"That sounds great."

"Good, it's settled then, dinner Sunday night at six. Now, let's get you to your room so you can get ready for social hour." She lifted my suitcase and bustled up the stairs.

I attempted to keep pace with Cora but found I stayed a couple of steps behind her. My thighs tightened with each step and I regretted not keeping up with my workouts.

Cora was already at my door and sliding the key in the lock when I made it to the top of the stairs. I stood for a moment and took in my surroundings. The landing was large enough it could have doubled as another room. The only piece of furniture in the space was a table under the window holding a vase of flowers. I imagined a much more inviting design for the open area; two chairs with foot stools separated by a small bookcase and a reading lamp, centered against the wall.

Plaques hung next to each of the six doors identifying the room number and the restroom. Directly across from where I would be calling home for the next three days was a red, numberless door with a doorbell mounted on the wall. I stared at the metal plate with the small black button in the center.

"That door leads to the third floor, where my husband, daughter, and I live. It is off limits. However, if it's after 9 p.m. and it's an emergency, you can ring the doorbell and I'll come down. Now, let's get you settled in."

"Thank you," I said.

She opened the door to my room and placed my suitcase by the foot of the bed. "*You* get one of only two rooms with your own private bath." I stood inside the entry and watched her walk into a small room. Her words echoed off the tiled walls. "We took a little space from the next room to add this bathroom."

I leaned forward to get a glimpse inside; a sink, toilet and tub were stuffed into the narrow space. Cora walked to the armoire and spread her arms as if she was a model showing off a brand new car. "This is where you can hang your clothes," she said.

She moved quickly past me to the other side of the room. "And you have a *fantastic* view of the backyard and your very own desk to write your article and your review of your stay here."

I swear I could see a twinkle in her eye.

"Well, that's all. Let me know if you need anything else," Cora said.

"Thank you, everything looks great."

"Be sure to come downstairs in," she looked down at her watch and gasped, "my pies!" Cora ran past me and down the stairs at a sprinter's pace.

I was about to shut my door when I looked up and saw half of a man's face staring at me through a cracked open door to the room across the hall, next to the stairs. I raised my hand and gave a little wave to see what he would do. There was no response. His stare was unwavering. I didn't want to wait any longer to see if he would make a move. I shut my door and made sure the deadbolt was in place.

The thought of his eyes on me like that made my skin crawl and goose bumps covered my flesh. I shivered as I pulled my cell phone out of my purse and called Olivia.

"So, how is it?" Olivia asked. The standard hello was no longer necessary. We talked so often it was as if our conversation never ended.

"Before I get to that, when I get home we're going to start walking every day again. I can't believe how out of shape I've gotten these past six months."

"That's what happens when you get a new job and put your work before your health."

"Yeah, yeah, I know," I said. I walked back to the door and checked to make sure it was locked.

"So, tell me about where you're staying," Olivia said.

"It's quaint and…well, the people are a bit different than I expected."

"Do tell."

I pulled a chunky turtleneck sweater, a black dress, and a blue silk paisley scarf from my suitcase and hung them up in the armoire. With only a handful of hangers, my pants would have to be folded and placed in the drawers. My silk scarf, another thirtieth birthday present, needed a hanger. "So far I have seen a young couple with tattoos of spider webs on their necks and piercings in places that look very painful. They seem nice though. Then there was this grumpy man that pushed past me on the porch knocking into my shoulder without apologizing. This was after he shut the front door as I was about to go in. The innkeeper is very…bubbly. Her daughter, who is less than hospitable, is beautiful and I am guessing a bit of a fireball. She had on some red pumps that could have stopped traffic. Then there's the Polo man."

"The Polo man?"

"He is gorgeous! He looks like he just stepped off a plane from Italy and he was wearing Polo cologne. The Polo man."

"Please tell me you didn't do anything embarrassing when you met him."

"No, I haven't properly met him yet, I just saw him. He was walking up the stairs. He did say hello when he saw me staring at him."

"Kate! You said hi back, right?"

"Of course I did. What are you implying?" It was a redundant question and one that made us both laugh. She had witnessed my many clumsy and awkward moments when meeting a man I found attractive. "Anyway, right before I called you I was about to close my door and I looked up and saw one of the guests from across the hall staring at me from his room. He had his door cracked open. I waved at him to see what he would do. A normal person caught being creepy like that would shut the door as fast as they could, but he just kept staring at me, so I locked my door and called you."

"Wow, how long have you - Leo, take off your cleats before you walk through this kitchen - how long have you been there?" Olivia asked.

"Less than an hour," I said. I walked to the window and leaned against the sill. "There's a meet and greet at five. I'll get to know everyone then. By the way, this town, this B & B, is amazing, just beautiful. I have a perfect view of the backyard. There's a small greenhouse next to several rows of rose bushes which, surprisingly, still have blooms." I pulled the small desk closer to the window and sat down to make sure I could look outside while I was writing.

"We'll have to come up there and visit when you're not working and school is out. Call me back after the meet and greet and let me know how it goes with Mr. Polo man. I have to go. Leo just left a trail of clothes to his room and is yelling for me."

"Okay...wait." A flash of light from the window caught my eye. I stood up to get a better look outside and saw a blur of silver slice through the air. I moved closer to the window, so close my nose touched the glass. "Wait, don't hang up yet. Oh my God! I think...no...um..."

"Kate, what is it?"

"Some guy in a baseball hat just hit a blonde haired woman on the head with a shovel! She fell to the ground."

"What? What woman?"

"I don't know. He's dragging her behind the greenhouse. Olivia, she's not moving. What do I do? She's..." I stood, staring, stunned at what I had just witnessed.

"Kate?"

"Olivia, she's wearing red heels."

CHAPTER 2

I ran out of my room and down the staircase as fast as I could. Thankfully, I made it down the stairs without incident. But as I rounded the end of the banister my foot slipped on the rug and I fell to the ground, coming within inches of hitting my head on the last step. My right leg and elbow thumped against the hardwood floor. Watson and Goose sat as still as statues in the living room doorway staring at me as I sat on the ground wincing in pain. The kind of pain that makes you hold your breath hoping it'll stop the agony. I was embarrassed enough the cats were watching, I was about to be even more embarrassed as the smell of Polo filled the air.

"Are you okay?" the good smelling man asked as he knelt down next to me.

"Yes, I just slipped." He wrapped his strong hands around my good arm and pulled me to my feet. "Thank you. I'm sorry, I have to go." I slid past him, accidentally - although, not so much - brushing against his chest.

I started for the living room, where Watson and Goose were still standing their ground, when I heard humming coming from the kitchen. I looked down the hall and saw Cora swaying to music as she placed a pie in a pastel pink box. "Cora!" I yelled. I hurried toward her, with a slight limp, and the scent of Polo following close behind.

"My goodness! You startled me. Are you okay? What's the matter?" Cora said.

"Where's your daughter?" I asked. I tried not to sound too frantic.

"Mindy? She's on her way to Atlanta to visit some friends. Why? Is something wrong?"

"I was looking out of my window and I saw a man in a baseball cap hit a girl over the head with a shovel. She looked like...it could have been your daughter. She was wearing red shoes like the ones Mindy had on and she had long blonde hair," I said.

"It couldn't have been Mindy," Cora said, shaking her head. "She left a little while ago. But if there's a girl out there and she's hurt we need to help her." Cora untied her apron and tossed it on the island.

"We need to call the police," I said.

"Let me go outside and check on the situation first," Cora said.

"I'll go with you," the Polo man said.

"Thank you, Donovan," Cora said.

"I'll go too," I quickly added. "I can show you where it happened. Besides, it's better if we go out there as a group, the guy's probably still out there."

"No, Kate, you stay here. Donovan and I will go. You need to sit down and have a glass of water. You look flush. All this excitement has gotten you too upset. We'll be right back," Cora said.

I knew she meant well, but really, how did she expect me to act? Oh, hey, guess what? *Some guy just killed a girl in the backyard and I think it's your daughter. What's for dinner?*

"Really, Cora, I'm okay." I didn't wait for a response; I headed out the back door.

I stopped and did a quick survey of the covered patio, making sure the man wasn't lying in wait. I noticed a wicker couch and chair and a white patio table all cushioned in the same blue willow pattern fabric as the kitchen. There was no sign of the man or the girl. The patio would have been a cozy place to sit with a cup of cocoa, any other time than the present.

Donovan and Cora passed by me and made their way to the back of the yard where the rose garden bloomed. My leg throbbed where a nice size bruise was forming, but I didn't let it stop me from keeping pace with Donovan. Cora was a different story. Her short legs carried her fast and abruptly to the far left of the yard where a covered bench faced the rose garden. I started to yell out to Cora to let her know she was going the wrong way when Donovan grabbed my attention.

"Where did you see it happen?" Donovan asked.

"Over there." I pointed to the back corner of the yard where a frosted Plexiglass greenhouse sat. A surge of terrified excitement came over me. What if she was behind the building lying in a pool of blood? What if the killer was back there? I craned my neck to see if I could see the man in the cap or the blonde woman, but we were too far away.

I glanced over at Cora. She was bent over looking at a rose bush containing several light pink blooms. She wasn't in a frantic search for her daughter or whoever the woman may be. Cora literally smelled the roses. I stood in awe and watched her slide her fingers under a bloom and straighten it to get a proper whiff.

"You ready?" Donovan asked.

The garden was made up of six rows of bushes with stones in between each row allowing visitors to get up close and personal with each flower. We stood at the edge of the last row like two kids ready to dive into the deep end of a pool for the first time.

"Yeah," I said.

Donovan took careful, slow steps on the stone path between the bushes that led to the back of the property, marked by a white picket fence that matched the one in the front yard.

Cora walked along the slender path between the roses and the fence line, meeting up with me and Donovan as we stepped onto the browning grass. She pushed past Donovan and took several strides toward the greenhouse. The back of the building jutted out several feet past the garden and was a little more than a coffin's width from the fence. From our vantage point we were still unable to see if the victim or criminal were back there.

"Wait," Donovan said to Cora. He reached out and touched her arm to stop her from going any further. "Whoever did this might be hiding back there, let me go first. And be careful where you walk so we don't disturb any evidence."

I was impressed. He was handsome and chivalrous.

We kept in sync with Donovan, staying behind him until we were close enough to see behind the greenhouse. We stood there, staring at the same thing. Nothing. Absolutely nothing.

Cora and Donovan looked at me with furrowed brows. The greenhouse was pushed deep into the corner of the yard leaving room enough for only one person to squeeze between the building and the fence. There was nowhere to hide, nowhere to escape. Where was she? Where was he? A chilled breeze swept across my sweaty palms.

Cora walked to the front of the building. She went to open the door but the padlock was still in place. "I don't have my key with me to open the lock." She cupped her hands over her face and looked hard through the frosted glass. "I only see shadows of plants and tables. Kate, are you sure this is where you saw it happen?" Cora asked.

"I'm positive. It happened right here." I pointed to the grassy spot behind the white rose bush where Mindy stood. "Then he dragged her over this way," I said, showing them the direction the perpetrator took her. Their eyes veered to the backside of the greenhouse.

"Where were you when you saw it happen?" Donovan asked.

"I was in my room." I moved to the other side of Donovan and aimed my finger at my window. "I was right there." I looked over and saw a man in the hall window looking down at me. It looked like the same face I had seen peering at me through his cracked open door, when I was shown to my room. I turned to Donovan and Cora to ask them if they could see the man as well, but they had turned back around and were investigating the space behind the greenhouse. I glanced back at the hall window and watched the man move out of sight.

"Well, I'm not seeing anything at all, Kate. Maybe you just thought you saw something happen," Cora said. "You're probably just tired from the long drive up here."

I turned to face her. "It wasn't a long drive. I know what I saw," I said. "She had blonde hair and was wearing jeans and red high heels and...it was right there. She was standing like this." I walked to the last rose bush in the row and bent over to smell the white blooms the same way the girl did. "And when she started to straighten up the man hit her over the head with a shovel. She fell to the ground and he dragged her behind the greenhouse by her arms." I moved back to the edge of the building. "Her shoe fell off right there and..." I felt Cora touch my arm.

"Did you see her face?" Cora asked.

"No, her hair was in the way," I said.

"What did the man look like?" Donovan asked.

"He was tall, thin, and he was wearing a hunter green coat and baseball cap, but I couldn't make out his face." But I could see the looks of doubt on their faces. "I'm not making this up. I just don't understand how or where..."

"I'm sure you did see something, dear. Why don't you go take a hot bath and get ready for social hour? It'll make you feel better." Cora smiled and urged me along. "I'll call Mindy and make sure she's okay. I think that will make both of us feel better."

I looked at Donovan who gave me a crooked smile and a shrug.

I didn't need to feel better. I didn't feel bad. Frustrated, yes. Confused and a bit freaked out, yes. But not bad. I did agree with her about one thing though, a bath would feel good.

I could hear muffled voices coming from

downstairs as I made my way to my room. I imagined Donovan and Cora were discussing whether or not they should call a psychiatrist for the crazy woman in room four.

I stopped short of opening my door and looked back at the room across the hall to see if I was being watched. I was relieved when I saw the door closed. I walked to my bedroom window and stood in the exact same spot I was when I was talking to Olivia. I pulled out my phone and took a couple of pictures of the backyard.

Did I imagine the whole thing? Doubt started to spread through my mind but I put a stop to it immediately. I couldn't have imagined something like that happening. I know what I saw. What I couldn't figure out was how someone could knock someone out, move the body and leave no trace of ever having been there in less than fifteen minutes.

The throbbing in my head now matched that of my leg. I turned on the bathtub faucet and ran my fingers over the small lump on my thigh. I tested the water temperature with the tips of my fingers then poured a few drops of complimentary rose oil and Epson salt in the bathtub. I let my body sink into the soothing water. The oil seeped into my body leaving my skin soft and fragrant while the salt pulled the pain from my leg. The bath relaxed my body but couldn't shut off my mind. I needed to talk to someone about what happened. I needed to call Olivia.

I got out of the tub and pulled my colored L'Oreal 6CB chestnut hair in a ponytail and put on a pair of jeans, a white sweater, and my blue paisley silk scarf. I finished off the outfit with a pair of flats and diamond stud earrings, then picked up the phone and called Olivia.

"Are you okay?" Olivia asked.

"I just...I don't know. None of this makes any sense."

"Murder usually doesn't, in my opinion."

"No, not that, well yes, that, but..."

"Kate, what are you talking about? What doesn't make sense? Are the police there yet? Are they questioning you? Did you see the body? I can't believe this is happening. Are you going to stay there or move to a hotel?"

"That's the thing, it's not happening. We went outside to where I saw the girl get hit and there was nothing. No body or any evidence anyone had even been back there. I can't move to another hotel. Everything is booked up and to be honest, I don't want to leave. I want to stay here and figure out what happened."

"Be careful, Kate. You said 'we went out there.' Who is 'we'?" Olivia asked.

"It was me, the innkeeper, Cora, and...you ready for this, Donovan, better known as Mr. Polo."

"So, he has a name. Donovan," Olivia said, extending the last syllable. "I like it."

"It fits him."

"I wouldn't know I haven't seen him. You know, you could pretend to be texting and take a picture of him and send it to me."

"I think I am going to avoid him for a while. When I went running out of my room, after I hung up with you, I slipped on the rug at the bottom of the stairs and fell to the floor. He witnessed the whole thing."

"You're kidding." I could hear her start to giggle. "Are you okay?"

"Other than the plum colored bruise on my leg, yes. "

She couldn't hold back any longer and a burst of laughter shot through the receiver. It didn't take but a second for me to join her. Every time a snort escaped her nose our laughter increased. My eyes stung with tears. I desperately needed humor to cut through the thick air of the past hour.

It took Leo asking Olivia when dinner would be ready to bring us back to our senses.

"You know, maybe I didn't see anything," I said.

"Don't doubt yourself. You're a rational person; you don't just go around making things up. Maybe you saw something happen but it wasn't what you thought. Go enjoy the rest of the night the best you can and in the morning revisit the events that led up to when you saw the girl attacked. Maybe you'll be able to make better sense of everything," Olivia said.

"You're right. I am looking forward to the festival and then getting some work done. I'm sure that'll take my mind off all of this."

"If you can't get what you saw out of your mind, as we both know you sometimes have a hard time doing, you could ask the other guests if they saw anything."

"I'm not bringing this up to them," I said.

"It's a little late for that. I'm sure everyone already knows. Trust me; I teach middle school kids, I know just how fast a rumor can spread. Listen, I have to get this endless eating machine some dinner, but call me later tonight and we'll talk some more."

"Okay. Oh, I forgot to tell you! Remember that guy that was staring at me through his door when I checked in? When we were out in the backyard I was pointing to my window to show Donovan and Cora where I was when I saw everything happen and that guy was standing at the hall window. He was looking at me, just me, with those beady eyes!"

"He was probably just interested in what you three were doing outside. But just in case, don't go anywhere alone. Bring Donovan with you. Call me later." Olivia hung up quick, before I had a chance to respond to her suggestion to bring Donovan with me.

I reapplied powder and lipstick then headed downstairs to meet the other guests. I stood in the doorway of the living room and surveyed the scene. The two cats, Watson and Goose, sat in front of the credenza with craned necks eyeballing the food spread. The tattoo couple whispered to one another in the corner of the room. The old lady was still sitting on the couch working her knitting needles and Donovan leaned against a far wall focused on his cell phone. I didn't see the grumpy man that ran into me on the porch, but someone else was there. Someone I wished wasn't. And he was walking right toward me.

CHAPTER 3

His beady eyes stayed fixed on mine as each step of his long thin legs brought him closer to me. I squared my shoulders, ready to confront him. He stopped in front of me and curled his lip in disgust then shoved past me and made his way through the foyer and up the stairs.

"That was weird," Donovan said as he walked up to me.

"You saw that too. He's been watching me ever since I got here. He was watching me when I checked in my room, when we were outside in the backyard, and just now. I don't know what his deal is." My pulse raced as I spoke.

"I'm sure he's harmless."

"I hope so," I said.

"Let's get some wine and hors d'oeuvres."

The credenza held an array of cheese and crackers, turkey slices, grapes, finger sandwiches, and shrimp cocktail on shiny silver platters. Tall glasses of sparkling wine flanked the end of the table.

Donovan handed me a small white ceramic plate with a gold leaf embossed in the center. My stomach told me to pile the plate high and eat like it was my last meal. My head reminded me there was a gorgeous man standing next to me. I debated what items to put on my plate. I planned on eating a delicious helping of unhealthy food at the festival and didn't want to fill up on the healthy stuff.

I must have been staring at the food for a long time because Donovan said, "Are you one of those women who eats three grapes and then talks about how full you are?"

"Ha, no, I plan on eating at the festival tonight and don't want to fill up before I go." I put a sample of each item on my plate then looked around at the other guests who were still in the same spots they were when I came downstairs. "I wonder how long this meet and greet is going to last."

"Hopefully not too long, I'd like to see what's going on downtown too," Donovan said, handing me a flute of white wine.

I followed Donovan to a set of chairs in front of the bay window, which gave us a panoramic view of the living room.

"Did you come here for the festival?" Donovan asked. He leaned back in his chair and crossed his ankle over his knee. He balanced his plate on his thigh, keeping it steady with his left hand, which happened to lack a wedding band. I focused on his ring finger in search of a tan line and was pleased the skin was equally bronzed.

"Yes, but for work. I write travel articles and I'm here reporting on the town and the festival," I said. I took a sip of wine and saw, from the corner of my eye, a furry paw reach up and swipe a piece of turkey from Donovan's plate, teetering the dish. I let out a short laugh sending wine bubbles up my nose. I coughed a couple of times before continuing. "What about you? Are you here for business or pleasure?"

"Did you just see that cat steal a piece of meat off my plate?" Donovan looked down at Goose who was licking his lips. "Furry little thief," he said and smiled.

"Welcome everyone!" Cora walked in with her arms spread wide and a smile so big her top and bottom teeth showed. "I am so glad everyone's here. I hope you've had a chance to mingle and get to know one another."

Silence.

"Okay, I'll start with the introductions while you enjoy the refreshments." Cora turned to her right. "This is Sidney and his new bride Betts." Cora motioned to the young couple with tattoos.

"Everyone calls me Sid," the young man piped up.

Cora nodded and directed her attention to the couch where the old woman sat, only now she had a plate of food on her lap and her knitting needles and yarn were on the floor by her feet. "This is Mrs. Betsy Brandon and this is her son, Billy."

I had been so caught up in talking to Donovan I hadn't seen my beady eyed stalker come back in the room. So, his name is Billy. Good information to know.

Cora walked to where Donovan and I were sitting. "This is Kate. She is a writer for *Travel in the USA* magazine! She is writing an article about our annual festival and her stay here at Harmony Bed & Breakfast. Very exciting. I can't wait to read what she writes. Next to Kate we have Donovan. He's an architect from Chicago. He is going to be designing a children's hospital in the next town over."

Cora walked back to the entrance of the living room just as a tall slim man was heading for the front door. "Come, come, come. Let me introduce you to everyone." Cora grabbed the man by the arm and pulled him into the room.

I recognized him right away as the grumpy man who knocked into me on the front porch. Only now his face was soft and his eyes were downcast. The irritation I felt toward him shifted to curiosity mixed with a little bit of compassion.

"Everyone this is Peter. He is here all the way from California. Isn't that exciting? Okay everyone, mingle, mingle, mingle."

As fast as he entered the room, Peter was out the front door.

"So, you're the one who said you saw someone killed in the backyard," a sarcastic female voice said.

I turned my head in the direction the comment was made - directly in front of me where Billy's mother was sitting on the couch. Her eyes were the same shape as her son's. Something about her made my muscles tighten and jaw clench. Her empty plate lay next to her on the couch and her knitting needles clanked together with each fast stitch. She cocked her head to one side and raised her eyebrows.

"Well, I just thought I saw someone get hurt. How did you know about that?" I shifted my eyes to Billy. "Did your son tell you?"

"Oh, heavens no, I didn't need anyone to tell me. I could hear you ranting in the kitchen. I'm sure the neighbors could too."

"Oh, Mrs. Brandon," Cora said and let out a little laugh. "Nothing happened to anyone. Trust me; there would be police all over the place if something had happened." Cora picked up a glass of wine and took a long swallow. "We don't need to talk about something that turned out to be nothing. Right, Kate?"

Why was Cora looking at me like that? I didn't bring it up. "Sure, Cora," I said.

Donovan leaned toward me and said, "Do you want to get out of here and check out the festival?"

"Yes, I do."

Donovan and I put up our plates on the credenza and were about to leave when Sid and Betts walked up to us.

"Did you really see something happen in the backyard?" Sid asked.

"At this point, I just don't know," I said. I hoped to put an end to the conversation before it began. I knew what I saw, and I saw a girl get assaulted, but now was not the time to get into it.

"There's something weird going on around here," Sid whispered. "We can't talk right now, too many ears, but meet us tomorrow morning on the back patio after breakfast."

"Mr. Conspiracy Theory over here," Betts said and rolled her eyes, then smiled. "We have to get going."

"Good night," I said.

Donovan opened the front door and gestured with his hand for me to exit first. Goose decided he wanted to be the first out the door. Donovan stuck his foot out just in time to stop him from crossing the threshold. He didn't have to block the cat for long. Watson darted up the stairs with his ears pulled back. Goose bolted up behind him. The chase was on.

It was a perfect night for a walk. The sky

was clear and the nip in the air justified more fireplaces to be lit. The light breeze brushed by the smell of burning wood. The aroma reminded me of a camping trip Olivia and I took not so long ago, and sitting in front of the fire roasting marshmallows.

"This is what fall should feel like," I said. "Not hot and humid, like what I was marinating in this morning. Not that I am complaining about living in Florida, it has its perks, but fall should be cool and crisp."

"I've only been to south Florida a few times on business. What part of Florida do you live in?" Donovan asked.

"The panhandle."

"I hear the beaches are beautiful there; snow white sand."

"They are, but telling you about them doesn't do them justice. You need to come and see for yourself."

"I just might do that," Donovan said.

I walked next to him in stunned silence trying to suppress a girlish giggle. I think I just inadvertently asked him to come visit me in Florida. And he, somewhat, accepted. My heart thumped hard against my chest at the possibility.

"Listen," Donovan said.

We could hear the band playing a jazzy rendition of "Georgia on My Mind" as we reached the top of the small bridge that connected downtown to the residential area. Strings of light bulbs hung from the trees giving the park a soft glow. Groups of teenagers huddled throughout the park while parents tried to round up their energetic children to keep them from running into the men and women strolling through the festival. Police cars were parked on each corner of the square to block oncoming traffic from driving in the outside lane and to provide more room for the overflow of people.

The smell of greasy goodness grew stronger the closer we got to the festivities. The aroma of the tempting treats made my stomach growl loud enough for Donovan to hear. He looked in my direction and grinned.

"So, you're going to be writing about the festival and the B & B. It could turn out to be a very interesting article with all that's already happened," Donovan said.

"Do you believe me? Do you believe I saw that girl…killed?"

"Actually, I do. The way you came flying down the stairs and the look on your face, I didn't doubt you. It is odd that there was no body or broken branch or anything back there evidencing a struggle," Donovan said.

"Yeah, I know," I said.

We stepped across the street and into the park. A cluster of teenagers walked side by side forcing me to step to the right and brush up against Donovan's arm. Once the loud group passed us, I took a couple of steps to the side to create a comfortable space between me and Donovan, although I wouldn't have minded walking closer to him.

"You ready to get something to eat?" Donovan asked.

"Absolutely," I said.

A row of food vendors set up in concession trailers offered hot dogs, burgers, gyros, and sausages for eight to ten dollars, no sides included. I grunted at the thought of paying that much for half a meal but it didn't stop me from grabbing a mouth-watering gyro. We paid for our food then stopped at another stand, conveniently located in the trailer next to where I purchased my dinner, and picked up dessert. A young couple with a baby stroller left the bench behind the gazebo just as we arrived. Donovan and I sat down before any passerby's could lay claim to the seat.

The juices from my gyros dribbled down my chin and I tried, somewhat unsuccessfully, to conceal the mess with a napkin. There was a part of me that didn't care the tzatziki sauce was dripping down my face and onto my forearm. My taste buds were in heaven and I knew things were only going to get better when I bit into the fried powdery goodness that filled the circumference of the plate I had balanced on my knees.

Donovan and I didn't talk as we ate, which we did in record time. He was engrossed in his hot dog, Chicago style; mustard, onions, sweet pickle relish, dill pickle, tomato, peppers, and celery salt on a poppy seed bun.

"That was amazing," Donovan said. He got up and dumped our plates into the trash bin a few feet away.

"We need to get up and walk around," I said. I turned away from Donovan and licked the last bit of powdered sugar from the tips of my fingers.

"You okay?"

"Yeah, I just ate too much."

We made our way across the park to the booths filled with paintings, photography, handmade purses, jewelry, pumpkins and jams, kaleidoscopes, and glass figurines. The last stand we came to called out to me and I stopped. A powder blue nineteen sixties typewriter sat displayed among antique clocks and cameras. I turned over the white tag hanging from the return lever: ten dollars. Sold!

"Hi, y'all! Do you see something you like?" The middle-aged woman asked as she smacked her gum and ran her eyes up and down Donovan. Her black hair sat on her shoulders and curled under. Her form fitting sweater and pants were the same shade of red as her lipstick. A two inch thick white belt showed off her small waist.

"I'd like to buy this typewriter," I said. I pulled a ten dollar bill from my pocket and handed it to her.

"That's a good choice, there." She pointed to my purchase. Her eyes diverted to Donovan. "I don't reckon I've seen you two around here before. Are you just visitin'?"

"Yes, we're staying at Harmony Bed & Breakfast," Donovan said.

"Well, I'll be! That's Cora's place. Are you two on your honeymoon or somethin'?"

"We're not..." I said, shaking my head. But I was glad she thought we were a couple.

"We just met today," Donovan said.

"Uh huh. I'm Fanny." She held out her hand as we made proper introductions. "Born Francis, but everyone calls me Fanny."

"It's a pleasure to meet you, Fanny. You have some fabulous things," I said, gesturing to the items in her booth.

"Thanks. You two are staying at Cora's, tell me, is it true that some lady renting a room there saw some guy attack Cora's daughter out in the backyard, but when they went outside to check there wasn't anyone back there? Just ain't right to do that to a mother, scare her and all. Ya'll two wouldn't know anything about that would you?" Fanny asked.

"Who told you that?" I asked.

She took a step back and admired her fingernails then pulled her eyes back to us. "Cora's daughter knows my daughter. They went to the same college. That's how Cora and I met. Well, actually we met awhile before that but when our daughters became friends we started talking more. Anyway, my daughter and Cora's daughter were supposed to go to Atlanta tonight to meet up with some friends. Mindy was supposed to ride with my Cindy, but then Cindy's boyfriend called in a tizzy talkin' about somethin' or another and she had to go to his house so Mindy couldn't ride with her or would have to wait to ride with her or something like that. Cora called me and started telling me..."

I had to stop her rant. "You talked to Cora?"

"Yup, sure did. You think somethin' happened to Mindy?" Fanny asked.

"I don't know." I shook my head. "Have you talked to Cora since your initial phone call to see if she got in touch with Mindy?" I asked.

"No. I had to set up my booth so I put my phone on silent. I tend to get side-tracked when I get talkin' to people."

"You should give her a call, right now, and ask her if she's talked to Mindy," Donovan said. "I bet it would make her see what a good friend you are, that you're checking up on her and all."

"Well, maybe I will," Fanny said. She sashayed to her purse and pulled out her phone. "Cora, honey, it's Fanny. I was callin' to find out if you ever got a hold of Mindy." Fanny's smile faded. "Uh huh. Okay. Yes. Well, don't you worry honey, she's probably somewhere she can't hear the phone ringin'. I bet you anything she'll be callin' you tomorrow fussin' about how many times you called her. Let me know if I can do anything to help you, honey. I'll call Cindy and see if she's talked to her. Okay, bye." Fanny hung up the phone and shook her head.

I looked at Donovan and whispered, "This isn't good."

"No, it's not," he said.

"Well, she hasn't heard from her. I sure hope there's no truth to what that lady said she saw. Cora loves that girl, she's her only child. Anyway," Fanny let out a quick breath and put her hands on her curvy hips.

"Hopefully she'll get in touch with her soon," I said. "We should get going."

"Come back tomorrow. I'll be bringin' out some more items you might like." Fanny's eyes stayed fixed on Donovan as she spoke.

"You have some great vintage pieces," I said. "I can't wait to see what you bring tomorrow."

Donovan scooped up my typewriter and nodded at Fanny.

"All right, bye-bye you two," Fanny said, waving her long red fingernails in the air.

Donovan found a spot on the grass near the gazebo and sat down. By the fifth jazz rendition of a popular country song the temperature had dropped considerably. I tried to keep warm by rubbing my hands and arms, but it didn't help.

"I wish I had something to offer you to keep you warm. You want to head back?" Donovan asked.

"Yeah, I'm cold," I said. Donovan helped me to my feet and slid the typewriter under his arm.

We spent the first couple of blocks of our walk in silence. The moon was full and bright and served as a large flashlight guiding us home. The end of my day was making up for the start of it and I couldn't stop myself from smiling.

"Let's start at the beginning," Donovan said. "Walk me through everything that happened."

And then the bliss was gone. Reality pushed her way back in. I went through each moment, from Peter knocking into my shoulder on the front porch to being on the phone with Olivia when I saw the assault take place.

"Do you know what you'll do now as far as the Mindy situation goes?" Donovan asked.

"No. It just really bugs me that we couldn't find her body."

Donovan raised his eyebrows and let out a short laugh.

"Wait, I didn't mean it that way," I said. "What I *meant* to say was I can't understand where he would have taken her. I'm going back out there to see if I can figure how he escaped with her or if there's a place he could have hidden with her."

"Want some company in your search?"

He wanted to spend more time with me. Who cares if it was to search for a nonexistent body? Inside I felt like a teenage girl getting asked to prom by the most popular boy in school. I hoped my face didn't give away my emotions, as it so often does. "Yeah, that would be great. We can go out there tomorrow morning after breakfast?"

"Okay," Donovan said.

I snapped my fingers in an "aha" moment. "We're supposed to meet Sid and Betts on the patio after breakfast."

"Ah, the secret rendezvous. I'd like to hear his theory about what's going on at Harmony Bed & Breakfast. We can look after we talk to them."

"Ok, it's a date then." Did I just call tomorrow a date? What is wrong with me?

The porch light illuminated the front of the Bed and Breakfast. I stopped at the front door and dug in my pockets for my key. I turned around to get better use of the light for my search and was met with Donovan's eyes. Our faces were mere inches apart. Was he going to kiss me? Was this that moment?

He slid his arm past my waist and slipped his key in the lock. He opened the door a couple of inches and stopped. We looked at each other and then turned our head toward the raised voices echoing through the foyer. Donovan opened the door another inch.

We stood silent, listening.

"I can't believe you kept this from me all these years," a man's shaken voice bellowed, a voice I didn't recognize. "Why? Why would you do that?"

"You knew all along?" Cora's voice cracked.

"Don't blame me, it's his fault," the accusatory voice of Mrs. Brandon said.

Something soft moved across my leg. I jumped back and hit my elbow against the door. I looked down to see Goose rubbing his body against my shin. Heavy footsteps stomped on the hardwood floors.

Cora knelt down and softly made kissing noises. "Goose, come here sweetie." He ran to her and she scooped him up in her arms. "I made it very clear that door was to stay closed!"

"I'm sorry, we were just coming in. We didn't see him," I said.

A man I hadn't seen before, no more than five and a half feet tall with a balding head covered in age spots, walked between us and out the door. He kept his head hung low like he had been defeated. Cora stood in the center of the foyer and looked at us with the face of a mother scolding her child then turned and ran up the stairs with Goose in tow and Watson on her heels.

I took my typewriter from Donovan and thanked him for carrying it. We were almost to the staircase when Mrs. Brandon spoke up.

"Going upstairs for a little lovin', are we?"

"What?" I said. I couldn't believe my ears.

"See anyone else get killed tonight, dear?" Mrs. Brandon said. Her words were filled with disdain.

"Good night, Mrs. Brandon," Donovan said. He was gracious but curt. He put his hand on my lower back and guided me up the steps.

"What was...?" I said.

He put a finger to his lips.

Donovan walked me to my door, but any thoughts of a kiss were long gone. My mind was stuck on what Mrs. Brandon said. "Why was she being so rude? What have we done to her?"

"I don't know," Donovan said. "But I have

a feeling Sid was right, there is something strange going on here."

CHAPTER 4

I placed my typewriter in the middle of the desk and stepped back to admire her. She was an object of beauty. Nothing about her was automatic. She was perfect.

I pulled myself away from my new purchase and flipped off my shoes, grabbed my phone and scooted on to the bed. It took several minutes of adjusting my pillows against the headboard before I was comfortable. Once I was situated, I began to glance over the pictures I had taken earlier in the day when I arrived.

The B & B looked so idyllic; golden and copper trees with stray leaves skirting their trunks, a dressed up front porch, and a waist-high white picket fence surrounding the property. I flipped through a few more screens until I came to the pictures of the backyard. I zoomed in on a couple of the photos to see if I could find anything out of place, maybe something I had missed during my investigation with Cora and Donovan. No matter how hard I looked, everything seemed be in place.

My mouth opened wide letting out a fierce yawn followed by a quick laugh. I was glad Donovan wasn't around to see my face stretch out to that degree, not that it was any worse than slipping on the rug and falling in front of him or my stomach growling loud enough for him to hear or being caught staring at him. I rolled my eyes at the thought and put the phone down on the bedside table next to a bouquet of white roses that I was positive weren't there when I checked in.

The plump blooms spilled over the edge of the tarnished vintage silver vase which was tucked slightly behind the lamp on the far corner of the table. I picked up the small urn and brought it close to my nose, inhaling deeply. The perfume of the blooms swirled around me. I twisted the container and examined the flowers from every angle. The layered petals were a vibrant white with one exception, a reddish brown stain on the underside of one of the petals. The blemish looked a lot like dried blood.

I took a second look at all of the other flowers in the vase to see if I could find any other discoloration. Satisfied the rest of the blooms were unblemished, I turned my attention back to the blotted petal and took a closer look. I didn't want to jump to any conclusions, but if it wasn't blood, what else could it be? After a moment of deliberation and coming up with no other explanation, I decided it had to be blood. The question now was, why was there blood on a rose and who did it come from?

I slid off the bed and walked to the window with the vase still in my hands. The clouds had shifted and were hiding the moon. The light from the patio was off making it impossible to get a good view of the garden. But I was pretty sure the bouquet I held came from the rose bush Mindy was leaning over when she was attacked; the same rose bush I leaned over when I was showing Cora and Donovan what I saw happen from my window. If that was the case, and I would verify they were from the same bush in the morning, this could be Mindy's blood.

I felt a rush of adrenaline flow through my veins. This was evidence. My excitement was quickly stifled when I remembered there was no blood outside, there were no broken branches, no divots in the grass from where she was pulled...there was nothing. The stain could have simply come from a pierced finger when the blooms were cut off the bush. Then again, a thorn prick wouldn't produce a nickel-size patch of blood, would it?

I gently placed the vase back on the table, slipped on my shoes, and walked next door to Donovan's room. I lifted my arm, ready to knock, but stopped before my knuckles rapped on the wood. Maybe I could wait until morning to tell him about the rose? I stood for a moment contemplating the urgency of the situation and decided I couldn't wait. I had to tell someone. I tapped lightly on the door. A part of me didn't want to wake up Donovan if he was already asleep; another part of me wanted him to hear me no matter what he was doing. I knocked again, this time with a bit more momentum.

Donovan opened the door still dressed in the clothes he was wearing when we parted ways for the night, only now his shirt was unbuttoned showing off his solid, tanned chest. "Is everything okay?" Donovan asked. He slid the tiny white buttons in their slot while keeping his blue eyes fixed on mine.

"Um...hi." *Focus Kate.* "I'm glad you're up. I have to show you something in my room."

He cocked his head to the side and gave me a crooked smile.

I could feel my face heating up. "No, I'm serious, come on." I grabbed his hand and pulled him into my room.

"Kate, I'm flattered, but I think we should get to know each other a little better first." He was teasing me and I was enjoying it.

"Come here," I said, motioning for him to join me at the nightstand. "Look." I pointed to the vase.

"They're very pretty."

"No, look," I said. I picked up the vase and held it high enough he could see the brownish red spot on the underside of the rose.

"What is it?" Donovan asked.

"I think it's blood. I'm pretty sure these are from the rose bush Mindy was leaning over when she was hit on the head."

Donovan took the vase from me and brought the flowers closer to him. "Yeah, it looks like it could be blood or..."

"Or?"

"I don't know. Dried mud or rust from wet clippers," Donovan said.

"But it could be blood," I said.

"Yes, it could be."

I let out a heavy sigh.

Donovan tilted his head to the side and crinkled his forehead. "Mindy was attacked after you checked in. The roses were already in your room, so it can't be Mindy's blood."

I shook my head. "They weren't in here when I checked in. I think someone, maybe Cora, put them in here when we were at the festival."

"Why?" Donovan asked.

I shrugged and said, "Maybe she forgot to do it before I arrived."

Donovan fixed his eyes on the flowers. "Are you sure they weren't in here before everything happened?"

"Yes. What do you think I should do?"

He paused for a moment before answering. "Pull the flower with the blood on it out and hide it somewhere you don't think Cora will find it when she comes in to clean. Put the rest of the flowers back where you found them. We can examine them more in the morning." Donovan handed me back the vase. "I was about to go downstairs and get something to drink. You want to join me?"

I tried not to smile too big. "Let me do this real quick then we can go down." I wrapped my finger around the stem of the rose and slowly pulled it out of the vase, careful not to disturb the evidence. Several other blooms tried to join the tarnished rose as I pulled from the container and I had to tuck them back into their original position.

I scanned the room in search of the best place to hide a flower. Inside the wardrobe was an option, but something about keeping a bloody rose near my clothes gave me goose bumps. The desk was a better alternative. Two small, empty drawers flanked the long slender center drawer which contained several office supplies. I gingerly laid the rose down in the very back of the drawer and placed a block of notepads in front of it.

"Okay, I'm ready," I said.

The lamp on the desk in the foyer gave off a comfortable glow and provided enough light for us to navigate our way down the stairs. As we passed the living room I noticed the faint smell of burned wood. I poked my head in the room to see if Mrs. Brandon was still knitting and braced myself for her next comment. Glowing embers were all that remained and the room had a sense of warmth again.

I caught up with Donovan, who was half-way down the hall to the kitchen. He flipped on the light switch illuminating the white walls and stainless steel appliances. It took a second for my eyes to adjust, but once they did they focused on a plate of chunky chocolate chip cookies covered with cellophane on the center of the island.

Salad dressing in glass bottles clanked against one another as Donovan opened the refrigerator door to pull out two bottles of water. He handed me one and walked to the kitchen table. He sat in one of two chairs. I debated whether or not to sit next to him or across from him on the built in bench. He made the decision easy when he stood up and pulled out the chair next to his and offered it to me. I gladly accepted.

"This has been one of the most, I don't even know the word to describe today," I said and took a sip of water.

"Very true," Donovan said.

"It's weird that the flowers just showed up in my room, isn't it. I mean, this late in the evening."

Donovan shrugged. "Maybe it's like you said, Cora forgot to put them in there before you got here and saw an opportunity to do so when you were gone."

"I suppose so. Still, I'm curious what that spot is on the rose. I really think it's blood." I took a drink of water and moved on to my next thought. "When we were outside in the backyard, earlier today, did you see Billy watching us from the hall window?

It was kind of creepy."

"He does seem to watch you a lot. I can't really blame him," Donovan said and winked at me.

The heat rose in my face again. I blushed so much around him he probably thought I had a skin condition. He had confidence without any trace of arrogance. A trait I found very attractive.

"So you've noticed it too," I said.

"Yeah, I think he has a crush on you. He's probably harmless, but just in case I'm wrong, let me know if anything weird happens, okay?" Donovan said.

"I will, I promise." I said.

"I had a good time at the festival tonight."

"Me too," I said. "So, what do you think they were arguing about when we..." my mouth froze in mid-sentence and I turned to face the entrance of the kitchen. I heard the front door close and voices bounce off the foyer walls. I looked at Donovan then back at the kitchen entry. The same laughter mixed with snorting I heard on the front porch this morning when I arrived echoed down the hall and I knew right away it was Betts and Sid.

"Hey! What are you guys doing in here?" Sid asked.

"Just talking. Where did you guys go off to tonight?" I asked.

"We went to my mom's." Sid sounded less than thrilled as he looked in the refrigerator and grabbed a couple cans of soda.

"It was fun," Betts said and joined us at the table. "As a matter of fact, Sid's mom had some very interesting things to tell us tonight."

"Your mom lives here?" Donovan asked.

"Yeah," Sid said as he scooted across the bench next to Betts.

"We're living in Auburn until we finish school, then we'll move back here," Betts said.

"Or to Atlanta," Sid said.

"Or here," Betts continued. "We're still discussing it."

"What interesting things did your mom tell you?" Donovan asked.

Sid leaned across the table and lowered his voice. "I was telling my mom what happened here earlier today. About how you saw someone get killed and all."

I cringed. Olivia was right, rumors only have one speed; fast. I imagined by the time I went back to the festival in the morning the whole town would know about the incident that may or may not (depending on who you talk to) have taken place here. I could only hope they wouldn't know I was the one who witnessed it.

Sid continued, "I told her about you guys and that sad looking guy Cora made come in the living room during social hour. She didn't know who he was but then I told her about Mrs. Brandon and her son. Man, her eyes got really big. So I was like, what? And she was like, Mrs. Brandon grew up here but when she was twenty two she got knocked up by some guy. She comes from money and status and her family was all upset because she wasn't married. They told her to marry him or she would have to leave town until after the baby was born. And if she came back here it would have to be without the baby. She left and never returned..." Sid paused for effect and leaned back against the bench, "until now." He gave a satisfied smile.

"Wow," I said. "So she split off from her family and had the baby. That's a brave thing to do, especially back then."

"Yeah, but she gave the baby up," Betts said.

"Then why didn't she come back sooner?" I asked.

"Because the guy who got her pregnant left town, with his new wife, her former best friend, and word got out about her situation. My guess is she was too embarrassed to come back," Sid said.

"How do you know she put the baby up for adoption?" Donovan asked.

"Someone knows someone whose grandma used to work at an adoption agency in Atlanta and she recognized the name because of all the rumors and their family and all," Sid said. "The whole town found out pretty quickly. A few years later Mrs. Brandon married Mr. Brandon, a rich guy from New York. Mom said her parents put it in the local paper. Six months later Billy was born."

"Did your mom have anything to say about Cora and her daughter?" Donovan asked.

"Or Cora's elusive husband?" I added.

"Mom said she heard some people in town talking about how Cora's going to be a grandma soon, but she said that's just old lady talk and she's not sure if it's true. The older people around here don't like Mindy because she dates married men. She didn't say anything about Mindy's dad other than he was smart to take a job where he was on the road most of the time."

"I wonder if Mindy got pregnant by some

married guy and he killed her when he found out," I said.

"Or the wife of one of the husbands dressed like a man and killed her." Sid's voiced echoed through the kitchen. "What do you think about that?"

"Shh, you'll wake the whole house," Betts said. "And that's just ridiculous."

"It happens, I've seen it on TV," Sid said.

"Anyway," Betts said. She rolled her eyes and smiled.

"When Donovan and I got back from the festival we walked in on Mrs. Brandon, Cora, and some guy we'd never seen before, arguing," I said. "He was too old to be someone a twenty-something would have an affair with though. Then again..." I shook my head at the thought.

"What were they arguing about?" Betts asked.

"We only heard snippets," Donovan said. "There was something about keeping a secret and blaming someone for not telling them something or another."

"Oh, man. You think it had something to do with the rumor Mindy's pregnant?" Sid said. "Or maybe it was about..."

"What are y'all talking about?" We turned in unison and saw Cora standing in the doorway.

Her hair was pulled off her face with a white head band and her fuzzy white slippers matched her tightly cinched robe. Her face was clear of makeup revealing blotchy skin. I wasn't sure if she looked like that from crying or if it was years of sun damage.

I knew we were all thinking the same thing,

how much had she heard?

"We were just talking about our visit with my mom," Sid said, waving his thumb back and forth between him and Betts.

"Whatever," Cora said, unconvinced. Her feet scratched against the tile like sandpaper against wood as she shuffled to the counter and placed a cup in the Keurig coffee maker. Her eyes stayed fixed on the stream of dark liquid as it filled her cup.

I wanted to ask her if she'd heard from Mindy since this morning. I looked around the table for encouragement. Betts kept her eyes fixed on her drink as she twisted the earring under her lip. Sid picked at a scab on his arm. Donovan had his eyes fixed on Cora.

I took a breath of courage and asked, "Cora, have you heard from Mindy?"

Cora turned her head in slow motion. Her eyes sagged like a sad puppy. I couldn't hear the word come from her mouth, but I knew what she said; no.

I started to tell her not to worry, everything would be okay. It was instinctively the first thing people said to someone else when they were going through a hard time. Only, I couldn't tell her not to worry. She had every reason to be worried.

I tried to think of something to say that would be of some comfort, but nothing came to mind. All I could get out was, "are you okay?"

Without answering, Cora shuffled out of the kitchen, turning off the light as she left.

We stayed still and quiet in the dark, keeping our eyes on the doorway, until we couldn't see or hear her any longer.

"I'll turn the lights back on," I said. I stood

up and glanced out of the window leading to the backyard. It was pitch black with the exception of a small circle of light encased by a halo bobbing on the far side of the yard and heading straight for the greenhouse.

I ducked down below the windows. "Get down," I whispered. "There's someone in the backyard."

"What?" Donovan said.

Betts and Sid slid down in their seats until their heads were below the window sill. Donovan crouched down next to me. His knee touched mine and a tingling sensation ran up my spine.

Sid turned around and poked his head up high enough to see outside. I didn't want to move away from Donovan but curiosity was pulling me to the window like a magnet. I made my way to the bench and sunk down on my knees next to Sid. Donovan followed suit and was soon beside Betts.

The beam from the flashlight lit a path along the back fence and then faded when the person holding it went behind the building.

"Does it look like it could be the same person you saw earlier today?" Donovan asked.

"I'm not sure. It could be. I need to see him again." As soon as the words came out of my mouth the man stepped out from behind the building. He was wearing a baseball cap and his height and thin frame seemed similar to that of the man I saw earlier in the day, but I didn't get a good enough look to be certain.

We eyeballed him as he walked to the other side of the yard. Our faces were so close to the window our breath fogged up the glass. I used my hand to wipe away the steam and saw him stop in front of the bench Cora had inspected earlier in the day.

"Where did he come from?" Sid asked.

"I don't know," Betts said. "What if he comes up to the house? What'll we do?"

"We run out of here as fast as we can," I said.

"He'll see us," Betts said.

The man started back across the yard waving the flashlight along the grass like it was a metal detector. Without any indication he was about to change direction, he raised the light to eye level and brushed it across the patio. We ducked in unison and sat on our heels. I prayed he didn't see us. I had to take deep breaths to slow my racing heart. We waited for the light to disappear from above our heads and then we slowly pushed back up on our knees to get another look outside.

His pace had picked up and he was on the far side of the yard. Any chance to see his face was almost gone. A few more steps and the only view I would have of him would be his backside.

Luck was on my side; he had an itch. He lifted his baseball cap and used the hand holding the flashlight to scratch his forehead. The light shone across his face for only a second, but it was long enough. It was Peter. Knock-me-in-the-shoulder, doesn't speak to anyone Peter.

A few feet more and he rounded the far side of the house. He was out of sight. We turned away from the window and let out a collective sigh.

Why was he in the backyard in the middle of the night walking around with a flashlight? I couldn't help but think he was a very troubled man. But was he troubled enough to kidnap or kill someone?

Sid hurried across the kitchen and flipped on the light switch.

"Try to act natural," Betts said to Sid.

"Grab the cookies off the island," I said as I sat back in my seat.

Sid wrapped his hands around the edge of the plate of chocolate chip delights and was about to head back to the table when we heard the front door open. Sid glanced down the hall before rejoining us.

"Who was it?" Betts whispered.

"Peter. He came in and ran up the stairs like he was in a hurry. I told you something weird was going on in this place," Sid said.

"Do you think he saw you look at him?" Betts asked.

"Nah," Sid said.

"Why do you think he was back there?" I asked.

"Looking for the body or clues," Sid said. "I bet he did it and he's making sure he's covered his tracks."

Betts' face crinkled. "What are you talking about? Why would he look for the body or clues if he's the one who did it?"

"Everything happened so fast this morning," I interrupted. "It really could have been anyone."

"Do you think maybe she was just knocked out and not killed?" Betts asked.

I could hear the hope in Betts voice. I wanted to believe the same. "Yeah, I thought of that earlier, but I don't know. She fell pretty hard, but we shouldn't rule out the chance she is still alive and this is a kidnapping," I said.

"Has anyone called in a ransom?" Sid asked.

"Not that I know of," I said.

"We would have seen the cops around here if someone called asking for money," Donovan said.

"Unless the note said they'd kill Mindy if the cops were called," Sid said, grabbing a cookie.

"Do you think we should let the police know something happened?" I asked Donovan.

Donovan shifted in his chair. "No, we should let Cora call them. We don't have any evidence to prove anything happened, other than what you saw. Without any proof the police either won't believe you or they'll suspect you. If you call them you'll spend the rest of the weekend at the police station answering questions you don't have the answers to."

"Let's investigate on our own. If we find something then we'll go to the police," Betts said.

"I think that's a good idea and we should start with Cora," I said. "We really don't know anything about her and her family. All we know is she runs Harmony Bed & Breakfast and Mindy is her daughter who helps her on the weekends sometimes. We need to find out more about the family to figure out why someone would want to kidnap or kill Mindy."

"Yes!" Sid stood in excitement and sat back down just as fast. "I'll ask my mom if she has any more info."

"Okay. I was also thinking it would be a good idea to ask around town," I said. "But inconspicuously. There's no better time than now, when everyone is out and about enjoying the festival."

"How are we going to do it? Just go up and ask people what they know about Cora and Mindy?" Betts asked. "Won't they get suspicious?"

"No, we don't want them to know what our real objective is. You go at it like that and people will freeze up and then run and tell Cora someone is going around town asking questions about her and her family. If she found out we would have an even bigger mess on our hands," I said.

"So, what's the plan then?" Betts asked.

We sat in silence for a moment. My mind weaved through scenarios and sly ways to snoop. I was pretty sure everyone else was doing the same thing.

"I've got it," I said to blank stares. "I'm writing an article and you're helping. We go downtown and talk to the locals at the surrounding businesses. We tell them we're doing research for an article for *Travel in the USA* about the festival and Harmony Bed & Breakfast."

"I'm in," Sid said.

"Me too," Betts smiled.

"Looks like you have yourself a crew of three," Donovan said.

"Okay, we'll work out the details in the morning, after breakfast."

I changed into a pair of silk pajamas then slid under the plush comforter. Every muscle in my body began to relax and I felt pleasantly heavy against the mattress.

The thought of Sid and Betts talking with childlike excitement as they went into their room brought a smile to my face. I was pretty sure sleep wouldn't come to them anytime soon. My mind turned to Donovan. Handsome, sexy, charming, Donovan. The pleasure that ran through my body took a turn and shifted to hesitation. Charming. Sexy. Ladies' man? Was he using his charisma and finesse to distract me from what was really going on? He is the one who suggested we not get the police involved. I pondered this for another moment then decided, no, he couldn't be the killer. He was in the foyer when I came running down the stairs and he wasn't as thin as the man I saw. It couldn't have been him. There was no way he could kill someone and one minute later be standing in the foyer without a speck of dirt or blood on him. Besides, he was helping me figure out what...

The phone buzzed and I was grateful for the interruption.

"You didn't call me back," Olivia said.

"I'm sorry. Things got even more exciting after we got back from the festival."

"Do tell! But start with the social hour," Olivia said.

I propped up the pillows against the headboard and looked at the roses next to my bed then across the room at the drawer that concealed the stained petal. I recapped the night for Olivia with a mix of excitement and suspense. It was eleven thirty when we finally hung up.

I closed my eyes ready for sleep to take me immediately. Instead, I saw the image of Mindy's body being pulled behind the greenhouse. It was as if I was watching a movie in slow motion. Was she really dead or just unconscious? Was Peter who I saw from my window? Why would he want to hurt

Mindy? Was he married and dating her?

My thoughts became blurred and I knew slumber was coming. I was almost asleep when I was startled by a clanking noise coming from across the room.

I leaned over and turned on the lamp next to my bed. I watched the door knob twist in slow succession. I pushed myself up and began to look for any sharp object within reach. I slowly opened the drawer to the nightstand. A black Bible, a note pad, and a pen lay side by side. The pen would have to do. I slipped out of bed and tip toed across the room until I reached the back side of the door.

Whoever was on the other side yanked on the door knob in a frustrated attempt to open it, but was denied by the dead bolt. I was sure the would-be intruder could hear my heart thumping against my chest. The person on the other side of the door gave a rapid twist of the knob and then stopped. I stood frozen. I could hear footsteps echo in the hall and then a door slam shut.

I released the air I had been holding in my lungs. I scurried around the room searching in every drawer looking for a more substantial weapon. The only thing I could find was a pair of dull scissors in the center desk drawer. I peeked behind the stack of notepads to make sure the rose was still there. It was.

I sat in bed and pulled my knees up to my chest and covered my legs with the blanket. I kept the red handle scissors next to me and my eyes fixed on the door, and waited.

CHAPTER 5

With the exception of a few birds chirping outside my window when they should have been sleeping, the room was quiet. It had only been an hour since the threat of intrusion, but it felt like an eternity. As the minutes passed and my blood pressure lowered I tried to think of any reason why someone would try to get in my room. Could it have been one of the other guests and they were confused as to which room was theirs? That was highly unlikely but possible. Maybe it was Mrs. Brandon's gentleman friend coming back for a visit and he went to the wrong room?

My eyes were wide open and I knew sleep wasn't coming anytime soon. I glanced at the desk drawer where the rose was still tucked away deep inside. Pushing the covers off, I walked to the desk and carefully pulled the flower out from its hiding place and placed it in my palm, blood stain up. The silky petals were in need of water. I wondered if keeping it hydrated would keep the evidence fresh or if keeping it moist even mattered. Just in case, I put the rose back in the vase and pulled the lamp forward to camouflage a portion of the flowers.

I grabbed my laptop and climbed back in bed. I pulled up a blank document and began typing:

If you're up for adventure come stay at Harmony Bed & Breakfast, where there's never a dull moment and you may just lose your mind.

    The minute you enter the picturesque town you feel a sense of comfort. However, once you cross the threshold of the town's premier B &B everything changes. People disappear, sweet looking little old ladies sit knitting while they stab you with spiteful words, and creepy men leer at you from behind slightly open doors.

    If you can get past all of that you can enjoy the beautiful, blooming rose garden, but beware, you may find a petal or two with blood stains.

    There is a silver lining though, and he smells like Polo.

    I sat back and admired my writing. Oh, how I would love to publish this article, but I wanted to keep my job so I pecked the delete button until all the words disappeared and then started on the short editorial for the "Happening Now" section on the *Travel in the USA* website.

    Two handfuls of travel writers worked for *Travel in the USA*. We each spent one weekend a month in a different location. The night we arrive at our destination we are required to post on the website's "Happening Now" section to let readers know the events that are taking place that weekend. After we complete our trip we turn in a full length article about the town or city we visited, to be published in the monthly magazine. Most of my assignments consisted of small town events, while another colleague traveled to the big cities, and another one wrote about weird and unusual adventures. Then there were the writers who focused on specific subject matters; wine, beer, food, art, and anything else that was trending at the time. The editor was constantly thinking of new ways to draw in readers and I had to admit, this was one of the most exciting jobs I ever had.

I downloaded the photos I had taken that morning of the girls hanging the banner and the band doing their sound check, and then began my short piece.

The small town of Harmonyville, Georgia is celebrating the tenth anniversary of their fall festival. The central park has been taken over by arts and craft booths, food vendors, music, and...

I saved my short piece then closed my laptop and laid it on the bed next to me. As soon as the screen of the computer clicked in its closed position, I went right back to thinking about the person who was trying to get into my room. I swung my legs off the bed, grabbed the scissors and walked to door. I put my ear to the heavy wood and listened. There were no footsteps, murmurs, or any sign of movement from what I could tell. With care, I slowly twisted the deadbolt until a small click let me know the metal had pulled away from the wall. I cracked the door open an inch at time, peeking out into the hall from behind it. Pale moonlight gave the empty space the appearance of a light fog.

I stepped one bare foot over the threshold and leaned into the hallway. I peered past Donovan's door to where the bathroom sat unoccupied. I checked to see if any lights shone from under any of the guest rooms. They were all dark. My shoulders relaxed and I went back to my room feeling a little better. But to be on the safe side, I double checked the locks to make sure they were secure. I placed the scissors on the nightstand and pulled out a competitor's travel magazine from my bag then crawled back in bed. I made it through the first fifteen pages, all advertisements, and to a promising article, but fell asleep a couple paragraphs into it.

The banging of the alarm's bells jerked me out of my slumber. I dragged my body into a hot shower then rubbed cinnamon pumpkin lotion over my arms and legs. I put on a pair of black jeans, boots, and a turtle neck. I topped off my outfit by putting on a long silver chain necklace with a black and white stone pendant and then pulled my hair into a pony tail.

I was about to head to breakfast when I saw the vase of roses from the corner of my eye. I pulled out the blood stained bloom and wrapped it in tissue. The delicate flower needed another hiding place. I thought about giving it to Donovan to keep in his room, but I wanted immediate access to it if I decided to take it to the police. I moved around my room in search of the perfect place to conceal the rose. I walked past the bathroom and noticed flakes of dust dancing in the sun light in front of the armoire. A curved ornate piece of wood attached to the top border of the decorative furniture added an extra four inches of height to the already tall piece. I stood on my tip-toes and swiped my fingers across the top. Dust particles floated down and coated my fingers. It had been a while since the top of the armoire had seen a cloth, making it the ideal place to hide the rose.

I locked my bedroom door and started down the stairs. A few steps into my descent and the smell of bacon, sausage, and pancakes hit me.

Four seats were occupied in the dining room. Donovan, Betts, and Sid sat at the end of the table, closest to the buffet, with Donovan facing the foyer. Peter took a seat at the opposite end of the table, as far away from everyone else as possible.

I made my way to the array of breakfast food. I pulled a white plate from the stack and covered it with two blueberry pancakes, two sausages links, and a generous amount of syrup. I grabbed a glass of orange juice and sat down next to Donovan, ready to devour my food.

"Did you sleep well?" Donovan asked me.

"Not really. I would have, but," I looked in Peter's direction and raised my voice, "someone tried to break into my room last night." I didn't know if it had been Peter who was on the other side of my door, but if it was I wanted him to know I was aware someone was out there and I wanted to see if he would react to my comment.

Peter continued to focus on his food while my three companions gave a collective "What?" and "Are you all right?"

"Yeah, I was up most of the night. I think it was somewhere around four this morning when I finally fell asleep."

"Are you sure you're okay?" Donovan asked. His voice was sincere and comforting.

"Yes, it just made me nervous."

"How do you know someone was trying to break in?" Sid asked.

"He was jiggling the doorknob and pushing on the door. It was dead-bolted so he didn't make much headway and gave up after a minute."

"How do you know it was a guy?" Betts asked.

"I guess I don't, but I highly doubt it was

Mrs. Brandon," I said, then lowered my voice. "And we all saw what state Cora was in last night." I raised my eyebrows and took a bite of my pancakes.

"Are you going to tell Cora?" Betts asked.

"No, she has enough on her plate and I couldn't prove it anyway. I don't know, it could have just been someone trying to get in the wrong door," I said, shrugging it off as if it was no big deal, but my gut didn't agree with my nonchalant attitude.

With a speed that even shocked me, I cleaned off my plate and leaned back in my chair. I rested my hands on my belly and let out a stuffed sigh.

"Was it good? Donovan asked, smiling.

"Yes. I was famished."

Donovan laughed. "I love how you are totally you."

"What you see is what you get," I said. He was watching me, paying attention to me, and he liked it. My pulse quickened at the thought. But I had to put Donovan out of my mind for the moment because Peter was finishing off the last bite of his breakfast and I knew it wouldn't be long before he left the room. I wanted to talk to him. I wanted to know what he was doing in the backyard last night. I wanted to know something, anything, about him.

"Has anyone seen Cora this morning?" I asked.

"No," Sid said. "All this was already set out when we got down here."

Peter wiped his hands with his napkin and tossed it on his plate.

"Peter, have you seen Cora this morning? Do you think she might be out in the garden?"

Donovan swallowed his coffee hard and Betts' brown eyes widened. Sid's head jerked in my direction then he turned to look at Peter.

Peter stood and picked up his plate and silverware and deposited them in the bin designated for dirty dishes at the opposite end of the room. He turned for the doorway.

"Peter?" I said.

He looked at me, his eyebrows folded together. I had clearly irritated him. Peter shook his head and hurried out of the room.

Donovan cleared his throat and gave me a devious smile. He leaned back in his chair and crossed his arms. Sid and Betts tried to stifle their laughter.

"What?" I said and shrugged. I tried hard not to smile, but was unsuccessful. "He hasn't said a word to anyone since he got here and I want to know what his deal is. What was he was doing outside in the dark with a flashlight? Was he the one at my door last night? Is he a mute?"

"I don't think it's going to be easy getting any information from him," Donovan said.

"I'm up for the challenge," I said.

"We could go check out the backyard and see if we can find what he was looking for," Betts said.

"That's my girl," Sid said.

"We could," Donovan said and took a sip of coffee.

"Have you guys seen Mrs. Brandon or Billy this morning?" I asked.

"No. Why?" Donovan asked.

Sid and Betts shook their heads.

"Just curious," I said. "Maybe it was Billy

who was trying to get in my room last night. I wanted to mention it in front of him to see his reaction. As far as Mrs. Brandon goes, after her snide remarks last night, I would like to stay as far away from her as possible."

"What did she say?" Sid asked.

"You know, the whole 'did you see someone murdered' thing," I said.

"Yeah," Sid said. "Are we still going to go around town and ask people questions for your article?" Sid raised his eyebrows and nodded in a - you-know-what-I-mean gesture.

"Yeah," I said. "But I want to take a look around that bench in the backyard first."

"Good morning!" Cora said as she entered the dining room. "Did everyone sleep well last night?"

I could tell the others were as confused by Cora's demeanor as I was. We watched her pour a cup of coffee from the community pot and saunter to the window. A smile broke out on her face as she looked outside.

"Cora, you're in a good mood," I said.

"You know, Kate, I am. I just know my Mindy is fine and in Atlanta with her friends. It was silly of me to think otherwise," Cora said. She turned around and glanced at me then back out the window. "Mindy will be home Sunday night. You'll see."

I couldn't help but wonder about Cora's state of mind. "So, you talked to Mindy then?" I asked. I knew she hadn't, but I wanted to see what had made her so convinced Mindy would be back.

"I don't have to talk to her. A mother knows when something is wrong with her child and I don't have that wretched feeling inside. You'll understand what I mean when you have children of your own. Stop worrying yourself and go enjoy the festival. I'm bringing some pies to Hailey's booth this morning. You should stop by and see her. She sells the best homemade preserves in Georgia."

Cora patted my shoulder and left the room. She called out for Watson and Goose, who appeared out of nowhere, to follow her upstairs.

"Okay, that was odd," Donovan said.

"Dude, what is up with her?" Sid asked.

I waited until I heard Cora close the door to her third floor apartment before getting up from the table. I poked my head around the wall and looked upstairs to make sure nobody was lingering in the hall. Once I was satisfied the coast was clear we headed to the patio.

"How do you want to do this?" Betts asked.

"Donovan and I will go to the bench. That seems to be where we're missing all the action," I said. "You and Sid split up. One of you can go upstairs and one of you can stay down here. Keep an eye on what's going on inside the house and if anyone looks like they're about to come outside, let us know. And make sure no one watches us from the hall window. I don't know where Billy is, but it seems like every time I turn around he's watching me. We'll only be a couple of minutes."

Betts and Sid went back inside the house and Donovan and I headed to the bench. A gust of wind pushed the scent of Polo across my face and I thought back to less than twenty-four hours ago and the first time I smelled him walk by. As we strolled through the grass I imagined what it would be like to have him by my side on a daily basis. I knew it wasn't possible, he lived in Chicago and I lived in Florida. Then again, he could fall in love with me and move to the Sunshine State. We could live on the beach and...I threw my hand up and grabbed the railing that supported the trellis around the bench to keep myself from falling into it.

"Are you okay?" Donovan asked.

"Yeah, just deep in thought," I said.

We sat down at the same time. Donovan leaned back, crossed one foot over his knee and rested his arm on the back of the bench behind my shoulders. It felt so natural. This was another perfect moment for a first kiss. All he would need to do is wrap his hand around my shoulder and gently pull me close to him. I would turn to face him, our lips inches apart, the look in our eyes, the knowing. This could be that moment. We would lean in, part our lips and...

"Kate? Kate?" Donovan said.

My gaze was on Donovan's lips when he pulled me back to reality. I shook my head and said, "Yes, I'm sorry. I was thinking about, um, never mind." I took a deep breath and changed the subject. "Okay, what could they have been looking for?" My eyes zeroed in on the small patch of dying grass at the base-line of rose bushes.

"I don't know. You see anything?" Donovan asked.

"No, and I don't see anywhere to hide anything either, but this is where they were both looking." I rested my elbows on my knees leaned closer to the ground. Donovan did the same. "Do you see anything?"

He shook his head. "It would be helpful to

know what we're looking for."

"Maybe we should rub our hands along the grass and see if we can feel anything?"

"The dead grass is pretty thinned out. I'm thinking we would see whatever it is that has caused so much interest."

I leaned back and looked up at the hall window. Betts knocked on the glass and waved her hand for us to come inside. "I think our time is up," I said and pointed to Betts.

I stood up, reached my arms above my head and pressed my feet into the ground, giving myself a full body stretch. Something hard pushed against the sole of my shoe. I moved aside and bent down to pick up a quarter size silver locket that was stuck in the dewy ground. I dusted off the dirt and noticed the chain was broken but the charm was still intact. I pushed my nail into the small notch and pulled the locket open. Two small, faded photos appeared. The faces looking back at us were unmistakable; Cora and Billy.

Donovan and I looked at each other. Why on earth would Cora's and Billy's photos be in the same locket?

"Hey!" Sid yelled from the patio. "You need to come inside now."

I slid the locket into my pocket. "Let's not mention this to anyone just yet."

"I think that's a good idea, at least not until we've had more time to process it," Donovan said.

When we walked in the house we saw Cora at the kitchen table, her face buried in her hands, sobbing. Betts and Sid stood behind the island looking a bit lost as to how to handle a weeping woman.

"Cora, what's the matter?" I asked.

"Mindy's friend just called. She said Mindy never showed up last night."

I had no words. Thankfully, Donovan stepped in.

"Tell us what we can do, Cora. How can we help?" Donovan asked.

"I don't know. I just don't know," Cora said through tears. "Mindy's friend Cindy called her and left her a message that she was going to her boyfriend's house and she needed to find another ride to Atlanta. Cindy never heard back from Mindy. When Cindy talked to one of their friends this morning they said Mindy never made it to Atlanta. Oh, God, what if she's been in a car accident?" Cora jumped up from the table and ran to a drawer across the room and pulled out a phone book. "I have to call the hospitals and see if she's been admitted," she said. Her fingers flipped through the yellow pages.

"Can you think of who she might have gotten a ride from?" Donovan asked.

"No," Cora said. "I'm calling the hospitals."

Betts and Sid joined us at the table where we were standing. "I feel terrible for her," Betts whispered.

We sat at the kitchen table and waited for Cora to finish dialing all the main hospitals en route to Atlanta. Each call ended with mixed emotions; relief and worry. "I'm going to go look for her. She may be stranded and her cell phone is dead. Maybe she's walking back here. Yes," Cora said more to herself than anyone else, "I'll take my pies to the festival on my way out. I can get the word out I'm looking for her that way. Someone has to know where she is." Cora walked out of the kitchen with three pink pie boxes stacked in her arms.

"Should we help her?" Betts asked.

"I wish we could," I said. "But I don't think her daughter is stranded on the side of the road. We might be more productive at the festival. When we get back we can see how Cora's doing."

Suddenly, a pained voice echoed through the house. "No, no, no!"

We ran out of the kitchen and were almost in the foyer when we heard Cora yell out. She stood at the top of the stairs, next to Billy, her hands smashing the boxes against her chest.

Donovan ran up the steps two at a time until he stood behind Cora and Billy outside of room number one. I stopped half-way up the steps. Billy threw his hands in the air and ran into room number one. Cora and Donovan stared inside the open door with expressions of dismay across their faces. Donovan turned and looked at me, then pulled his cell phone out, dialed three numbers and hit send.

I ran up the rest of the stairs and stood next to Cora. Billy's back was to us and he was bent over the bed. The nightstand held a pill bottle that was lying on its side next to an empty glass of water and loose petals that had fallen from a bouquet of white Oleanders rested on the ground.

The room consisted of two beds. The one on the far wall was still neatly made up. The bed closest to the door held the lifeless body of Mrs. Brandon; her pale outstretched arm hanging off the side of the bed and a blue paisley scarf wrapped around her neck.

CHAPTER 6

Billy frantically searched for a pulse on his mom's wrist. Not finding one, he let go of her arm. It bounced for a second on the edge of the bed and I had to swallow hard to keep the sick feeling in my stomach from coming up. Billy took a step closer to the headboard and leaned over his mother's face placing his cheek above her parted lips. He shook his head and slid the silk scarf away from her throat revealing small bruises. His fingers pressed against her flesh hoping to find any sign of life. When he couldn't find a heartbeat he stumbled onto a chair in the corner of the room and sobbed into his hands.

"Do you know what happened, Cora?" I asked. Betts and Sid stood wide eyed at the bottom of the stairs and waited for me to tell them what was happening. I lowered my hand to my thigh and held up my pointer finger letting them know I would tell them what was happening in a minute.

"You killed her! It was you! You strangled her with your scarf!" Billy stood up and aimed his finger at me as he screamed the accusation.

"I didn't kill anyone!" I yelled. Was he really accusing me of murdering his mother?

"That's your scarf," Billy said and pointed to her stiff body. "I saw you wearing it yesterday!

You...you..." Billy's face got redder with each word. He began to walk toward me with heavy steps.

My pulse sped up the closer Billy came to me. "What are you talking about?" A thin sheen of sweat formed on my forehead. I took several steps back, distancing myself from the doorway.

Donovan grabbed Billy's arm and pulled him deep into the upstairs hall mere seconds before he reached me. I turned and ran down the stairs.

"Where are you going? Don't try and run away!" Billy's voice echoed.

I held on to the banister as I hurried to the foyer. I pushed past Betts and Sid and made my way to the far wall. My head spun. I bent over and rested my hands on my knees and tried to catch my breath. Why would he think I killed his mom? I had absolutely no reason to harm that woman.

I needed some fresh air to help clear my head. I stepped out onto the front porch and sat in the rocker closest to the front door.

"Are you all right?" Betts asked, closing the door behind her and Sid.

"Not really," I said. "He's accusing me of killing his mom. Why would I kill her? I had no reason to kill her. And when would I have done it?" I rested my elbows on my knees and put my head in my hands. I fought to keep the tears at bay, but I could feel one escape down my cheek. I wiped it away quickly, hoping no one saw I was crying.

Mumbled voices and sobs from inside the house reverberated off the window. I felt terrible for Billy. What a horrible sight to walk in on. But to think I was the one who killed her, I just couldn't comprehend it.

"Don't worry," Sid said. "You didn't do anything wrong. There's no way the cops could think you killed her."

"Except for the scarf," Betts said. "Did you maybe leave it somewhere and Mrs. Brandon picked it up?"

"No," I said. "I took it off in my room. I don't know...I just don't know..."

It only took a few minutes from Donovan's call to 911 for two police cars and an ambulance to pull into the driveway. Two EMT's, one male and one female, got out of the ambulance and went to the back of the vehicle to gather their gear while four law enforcement officers headed up the walkway. Betts, Sid, and I hurried into the house to let everyone know the police had arrived.

Cora practically ran down the stairs when she saw the enormous man wearing a tan and green uniform duck through the front door to keep his Stetson from being knocked off.

"Sheriff Gathers! I'm so glad you're here," Cora said.

At over six feet tall and with a frame that spanned the width of the doorway, Sheriff Gathers' presence demanded attention. His hand swallowed Cora's as they embraced in a handshake that lasted a little longer than appropriate.

The Sheriff bent down and whispered in Cora's ear. I heard the bass of his voice, but he spoke too low for me to understand the words. Cora nodded and made her way upstairs. A moment later she was guiding a tearful Billy into the living room.

"She did it. She killed my mother," Billy's voice cracked as he said the words. He pointed a long, boney finger at me. "It was her, Sheriff."

"You," the Sheriff said, jerking his head at me, "go sit in the dining room." His gaze shifted to Betts and Sid. "You two go to the kitchen."

I had to step around the Sheriff, his deputies, and the EMTs to get to the dining room. I pulled out a chair, sat down, and waited.

A man carrying a brown tote came through the front door and joined the group in the foyer. After they greeted one another the Sheriff instructed two of the officers to accompany the medics and coroner upstairs. The remaining deputy followed Sheriff Gathers into the living room. The duo stopped in front of Cora and Billy who were sitting on the couch where Mrs. Brandon had been knitting mere hours ago.

I could tell by the way the Sheriff tilted his head he was giving his condolences to Billy. After he finished with his niceties, Sheriff Gathers straightened his head, pulled back his shoulders, and gave an order to his deputy who obediently ran out of the room and down the hall to the kitchen.

The top of my head started to throb and I rubbed my temples trying to release some of the pressure. I wanted Olivia here to tell me everything was going to be okay and we would get through this together. I wanted to sink into Donovan's arms and have him protect me. I wanted the weekend to start over.

From where I sat, I could see Billy's head resting against Cora's shoulder as she hugged and rocked him in her arms while they talked. What were they telling the Sheriff? Was Billy trying to convince him I killed his mom? Was Cora going to tell him about Mindy?

With nothing to do but sit and think, I closed my eyes and placed myself in front of Mrs. Brandon's bedroom door. I only had a brief look at the crime scene before Billy erupted, but I remembered seeing my scarf around Mrs. Brandon's blotchy neck and the mess on her nightstand.

There was a knocked over pill bottle and an empty glass. Could she have overdosed or had a bad reaction to her medication? There was a bouquet of oleanders by her lamp. Several petals were on the floor. Could there have been a scuffle and the petals were knocked off the stems? How did she get bruises on her neck? She could have been choking and grabbed her throat leaving marks. Maybe she died of natural causes like a heart attack or a stroke. I felt a bit of hope at the thought of plausible scenarios that could explain her untimely death.

When I opened my eyes I saw the deputy who was in the kitchen come down the hall and turn in my direction. I started to stand to greet him but quickly sat back down when the Sheriff bellowed from the other room. "She's mine. Go see what's going on upstairs."

I chewed on my nails and tried to still my bouncing knees. I needed to move around. I stood and walked back to the doorway and leaned against the casing. My body relaxed a bit when I heard the questions Donovan was being asked: Where were you when you heard Mr. Brandon scream? Did you know the deceased? What time did you go to bed?

"What time did you go to bed?" I said out loud to myself. If the police knew I was up during the hours Mrs. Brandon was killed, assuming it was one of the times I was awake through the night, they might think I had something to do with her death. Of course, the fact that she had my scarf wrapped around her neck doesn't help matters any.

"What information do you have about the disappearance of Mindy?" a deputy asked Donovan.

My breath caught in my throat. Cora must have told the Sheriff about Mindy and what I saw yesterday morning. Was she finally taking what I told her seriously?

"I don't have anything to tell you about her disappearance. One of the guests thought she saw her assaulted but when we went outside to check she wasn't out there," Donovan said.

"Did you call the police and report this assault?" another deputy asked.

"No. There wasn't anything to report," Donovan said.

"Who witnessed this supposed crime?"

Sheriff Gathers' cowboy boots pounded the floor as he walked across the foyer. I wanted to hear Donovan's response, but the Sheriff was closing in on me. By the time I reclaimed my seat the Sheriff was in the room. My fingers gripped the edge of the chair. I felt like a child about to be scolded.

A deep wrinkle puffed between the Sheriff's eyebrows. He leaned over me and locked his eyes on mine. "Let's take this outside."

I stayed a good distance behind the Sheriff as I followed him onto the front porch. A few of the neighbors had come out of their homes and sat on their verandas in an attempt to get a view of the events taking place at Harmony Bed & Breakfast. "Let the rumor mill begin," I said under my breath. I couldn't blame them; I would have done the same thing. But right now, I didn't want anyone looking at me and I didn't want to see them. I stood with my back to the railing and clasped my hands together in front of me.

"You have something you want to tell me." This wasn't a question.

"I'm not sure I know what you mean," I said in an attempt to stall the inevitable.

"Sure you don't. Okay then." He let out a deep breath and crossed his thick arms across his barrel chest. "Let's start with yesterday when you arrived in town and then you can tell me what you saw happen to Mindy. When you're done with that you can tell me where you were between nine o'clock last night and seven this morning."

I took him through each event, from the time I checked into the Bed and Breakfast to me, Donovan, and Cora going outside to look for Mindy. I intentionally left out a few key pieces of information. I didn't tell him about the blood stained rose I found in my room or the argument Donovan and I walked in on between Mrs. Brandon, Cora, and the mystery man, or the locket Donovan and I found when we did our own search.

"Uh huh," Sheriff Gathers said, nodding. He rubbed his chin for a moment then continued. "So, let me get this straight. You thought it would be a better idea to go investigate on your own, and tamper with whatever evidence there was, instead of calling the police?"

"There wasn't any evidence," I said, trying to steady my voice.

Sheriff Gathers widened his stance and

adjusted his belt buckle then put his hands on his hips. "Funny thing is," he said and leaned toward me, "no one has seen or heard from Mindy since you checked in here. And now we have this body upstairs with a scarf wrapped around her neck that I have been informed belongs to you."

"Yes, I know. Sheriff Gathers, someone tried to break in my room last night. Maybe it was the same person who killed Mrs. Brandon?"

"Someone tried to break in your room last night? How convenient. Maybe it was your new boyfriend, Donovan? I hear you two have been pretty cozy since you arrived."

"No," I said. "I don't know who was trying to get in my room. They twisted the door knob a few times and then left. It could have been..."

The Sheriff held up his hand. "I'll make a note of it."

"I saw a pill bottle on Mrs. Brandon's nightstand. Do you think she could have had a bad reaction to her medication? Or maybe she took too many pills? She could have died of natural causes like a heart attack or old age?" I said.

"Ms. Westbrook, why don't you leave the investigating to the professionals?"

"I didn't kill Mrs. Brandon. I know Billy said I did because she was wearing my scarf and yes, I could see bruises on her neck when he pulled the scarf away, but I didn't kill her."

The Sheriff tightened his lips and let out a strong breath from his nostrils. "He tampered with the body?"

"He was checking for a pulse."

The Sheriff shook his head and ran his

fingers across his forehead. "All right, when we look into the cause of Mrs. Brandon's death, if any evidence points back to you, you can be sure we'll let you know. Now, let's talk about Mindy. If you know something, young lady, you need to tell me because at this point things aren't looking too good for you."

I let out a heavy sigh. "All I know is I thought I saw her leaning over a rose bush and then some guy hit her on the head and pulled her behind the greenhouse. I was going to call the police, but there was nothing to call you for. When we went out there, there was no evidence a crime had taken place." I lifted my hands and shrugged my shoulders. I wanted to go on, to plead my case, but I could tell by the pulsing vein in his forehead it wouldn't do any good. The only thing I could think to say was, "I'm sorry."

His face relaxed and his shoulders lowered a bit. "I need you to stay in town until we get the autopsy results back on Mrs. Brandon. If you remember anything else, you let me know." He started to go back inside but stopped before opening the door and looked back at me. "You're not out of the woods yet. Don't leave town, understand?"

"Yes sir."

I looked over my shoulder to see if the neighbors were still ogling. They were. I wasn't ready to go back inside, but I couldn't stand being watched by curious onlookers.

I hadn't noticed how cold it was outside until I stepped in the foyer. The heat from the B & B wrapped around me like a blanket and my body tingled with warmth. I passed by the officers who were once again gathered in the foyer and made my way to the living room where Donovan, Betts, and Sid were standing silently by the window. Cora and Billy were still on the sofa, leaning on each other with slumped shoulders. I could tell by Cora's puffy eyes and red nose she had been crying.

I was almost to Donovan when Billy stood and said my name. I braced myself for another tongue lashing.

"I'm sorry. I shouldn't have yelled at you the way I did. I saw your scarf around my mother's...." Billy fumbled his words and the tears began again. He sank back down onto the couch and into Cora's arms.

"I don't blame you, Billy. I probably would have done the same thing," I said.

Donovan rested his hand on my shoulder. "How are you doing?"

"A little shaken up, but I'll be all right," I said.

"What did the Sheriff say, Kate?" Sid asked.

"He wanted to know where I was when Mrs. Brandon was killed and did I know her, stuff like that. The Sheriff asked me about Mindy going missing too," I said.

"They asked me about Mindy too," Donovan said. "I'm sorry Kate, I had to tell them about yesterday. I tried to keep your name out of it, but..."

Our conversation was interrupted by another eruption from Billy. "Why? Why did this happen?" he cried out.

"I don't know Billy, I don't know," Cora said, rubbing his arm. "What about my Mindy. I don't know if she's dead or alive or in a ditch somewhere waiting for me to..." she let out a noise from deep in her chest that sounded like a screeching goat.

Cora jumped up from the couch and ran to the foyer and wrapped her hands around the Sheriff's arm. Billy was fast on her heels.

"Wow," Sid said.

I turned back to Donovan and tried to regain my focus. "Don't worry about it. I told the Sheriff everything I saw and how we didn't find Mindy when we looked back there. But that's all I told him. I'm just glad the police know about Mindy now and are going to look into finding her. Did they mention how they thought Mrs. Brandon died?"

"No," Donovan said. "But I did hear Billy tell the police she had asthma and he couldn't find her inhaler."

"How do you think she got your scarf?" Sid asked.

"I don't know," I said.

"Do you guys think Mindy and Mrs. Brandon's murders are related?" Sid asked.

"I suppose they could be," Donovan said.

"I don't know if this is a good time to bring it up, but do you all still want to go downtown and ask people questions?" Betts asked.

"Absolutely," I said. I wanted to get as far away from the B & B as possible. "We need to take detailed notes about everything, even things you think aren't important. I also think we should work in teams. We'll work together." I waved my finger between me and Donovan. "You two stick together. I still have to write an article about this town so don't forget to ask questions about Harmonyville in general. Let's focus on the businesses around the park. Then around lunch time we can meet up and go over what we've learned and see if any of it will help us figure out what happened to Mindy. I don't know what to do about the Mrs. Brandon situation."

"We don't do anything," Donovan said. "Let's wait and see what else the police come up with and then we can figure out what action to take next. We can head downtown after the police leave here."

"I'm going to run upstairs real quick and grab my coat and do a quick search for my scarf," I said.

Donovan, Betts, and Sid stayed in the living room while I snuck past the police and upstairs to my room. It wasn't hard; Cora and Billy kept the officers busy as they took turns crying.

I pulled the heavy doors of my armoire open. All of the wooden hangers held an item of clothing and a jacket with the exception of two; the one that belonged to the turtleneck I was wearing and the one I hung my blue paisley silk scarf on. I felt tears welling up again. I hadn't said it to anyone, but I maintained a small hope that the scarf around Mrs. Brandon's neck wasn't mine. I hoped I would find it hanging in the armoire next to my dress and I could show the Sheriff and immediately be disentangled from her death. I couldn't let not finding it in the very first place I searched defeat me. I needed to keep looking.

I pulled open the drawers of the armoire. I sifted through my pants and night clothes but came up empty handed. *Don't panic.* Under the bed, it could have gotten kicked under the bed. I lifted the bed skirt and found nothing but a couple of dust bunnies. *Okay, now you can panic.*

I casually walked down the stairs with my

coat slung over my arm, and back into the living room. "Donovan," I whispered as I walked up to him. "My scarf isn't in my room. Someone must have gone in there and taken it."

I noticed Donovan's eyes look over my shoulder and a smile form on his face. I turned to see Sheriff Gathers watching us with a suspicious stare.

"We'll figure it out later. Right now play it cool," Donovan said.

"Look," Betts said, pointing to a black and white tail sticking out from under the Victorian couch, sweeping a section of the floor not covered by the rug. "Who needs a broom when you have cats?" Without warning Goose darted out from under the couch like he had been shot from a cannon.

Betts smile disappeared and we turned in unison to see why. The EMTs cleared the last step of the stairs and gently place the wheels of the gurney carrying Mrs. Brandon's body on the ground. She was covered in a white sheet, but I could still see the outline of her body.

The four of us walked to the edge of the living room and stood together in silence as she was rolled out of the B & B. As soon as the door closed behind the coroner Billy covered his mouth and let out a wail.

The Sheriff allowed Billy a moment to cry then cleared his throat bringing our attention to him. "No one goes in that room." He pointed upstairs to where one of his deputies was securing yellow crime scene tape on the door to room number one.

"Where am I going to sleep?" Billy asked through sniffles.

"Take it up with Cora," Sheriff Gathers said.

"I don't want anyone leaving town until after we get the autopsy done. Shouldn't take long, the morgue stays pretty empty in these parts. We can be reached at the police station if you need us." He turned and left the house with as much authority as when he had first arrived.

Billy's sagging eyes landed on Cora. "I think someone should have to give up their room for me. After all, it was my mother that was murdered and now I am all alone." Billy sniffled and added, "I need one with a bathroom." Billy looked at me. "I should get your room."

"Billy, please," Cora said.

Footsteps echoed from the hall. Peter stepped into the foyer. "He can have my room."

"Thank you, Peter," Cora said, relieved. "I'll be sure to set you up nicely in our bonus room off the kitchen."

Peter nodded and headed upstairs.

"Well, I could take the bonus room if there's a bathroom in it," Billy said.

"It is the size of a walk in closet. It has a single size bed and the bathroom isn't in the room. The room Peter is giving you has a king size bed and is almost the same size as your original room. It's the best I can do under the circumstances, I'm sorry." Cora said and headed back to the kitchen with Billy on her heals, complaining.

"All right, let's get going," I said. I threw on my coat and snatched two pens and two flimsy notepads with *Harmony Bed & Breakfast* embossed in gold at the top from the desk in the foyer. I handed out the writing instruments and pads of paper and exchanged phone numbers with Betts and Sid.

Something inside told me this was going to be a long day.

CHAPTER 7

A set of church bells echoed through the cool air warning us it was eleven o'clock. The festival was already overflowing with excited children and adults by the time we arrived downtown.

"Donovan and I will take the businesses on this side," I said, signaling to my right and continuing in a backwards L motion to the row of shops on the other side of the park. "You guys take the other two streets. We'll meet you where our corners intersect in an hour."

"You think that'll be enough time?" Sid asked.

"If you stay on track it should be."

"See you in an hour," Betts said and walked away with Sid by her side.

A wreath overflowing with sunset colored leaves, acorns, and ribbons hung on the door of In Bloom Florist. The bell hanging on the doorknob announced our arrival. The grey haired man behind the counter cradled a phone against his shoulder while he tied a bow around a vase filled with orange lilies and roses. He looked up, smiled, and raised a finger to let us know he would be with us in a moment.

The petite shop smelled of cinnamon and recently watered soil. Fresh flower arrangements filled refrigerated display cases that hummed and rows of glass shelves in the center of the shop were topped with Styrofoam pumpkins filled with fake flowers. Stuffed scarecrows, cinnamon brooms, candles, and a variety of plants were placed in between the arrangements adding to the spirit of autumn. A few balloons with a rainbow of strings attached to them floated to the ceiling in the far corner of the room.

I admired each carefully placed bloom and garnishment. I didn't know a lot about flowers, but the more I was around them the more I desired a garden of my own or, at the very least, to have a fresh bouquet of in season flowers in my home at all times.

Donovan leaned in close to my ear and said, "You're smiling."

"Am I?" I said. My smile grew wider. "I love this place. It's cozy. It reminds me of when I was little when we took trips to Connecticut."

"You'll have to tell me about that some time," Donovan said.

"Good morning!" the old man greeted us from behind the counter. "I'm so glad you're here. Do you see anything you like?" He carefully pushed the vase he was working on to the side and extended his hand.

"Yes. Everything," I said. "Hi, I'm Kate Westbrook."

"I'm Donovan," he said and shook the old man's hand.

"It's so good to meet you, Kate and Donovan. I'm Stewart Sanders."

I liked the sound of our names together and I held on to the thought for a moment before I began my standard salutation. "It's good to meet you too, Stewart. I'm here doing an article on Harmonyville,

Georgia for *Travel in the USA* magazine and I was wondering if I could ask you a few questions?"

"Wonderful! Ask away." He walked out from behind the counter. The sleeves of his white button up shirt were rolled to his elbows and his grey tweed trousers were held in place with a black belt and a small round belly.

"How long have you lived in Harmonyville?" I asked.

"I've lived here my whole life, sixty-seven years. As a matter of fact my family has been here since Harmonyville came about over two hundred years ago. This shop was my father's and before him his father's. The original building had brick floors. We've done a few modifications since then, of course. You know you have to keep up with the times. But I did keep some of its original charm." He led us to the side of the checkout counter and pointed out the original brick flooring. He then brought our attention to a framed piece of wood hanging on the wall behind the register with Est. 1889 carved in the center.

Once he started talking about his family and their flower business it was hard to get in any questions. Not that I needed to. He provided plenty of information for my article; unfortunately none of it would help in solving Mindy's disappearance.

I could have listened to him for hours, but time wouldn't allow it. "Stewart, what can you tell us about Harmony Bed & Breakfast?" I asked.

"That's a gem. You should go take a look at it if you haven't already," Stewart said.

"We're actually staying there," Donovan said.

"So you know Cora! She's a lovely lady. We

do business together," Stewart said.

"The B & B has a lot of character," Donovan said.

"I'm curious about the photos on the wall leading up the stairs," I said. "Do you know anything about them?"

"Well, let's see," Stewart said. "The people in the photos are the Harmond's. They were friends with my grandparents. Everyone knew everyone back then. They helped settle this town. Good people. Cora is doing right by that family. She was hired to take care of the house and collect the rent for several properties inherited by the Harmond's granddaughter after her parents passed away. Cora asked if she could turn the house into a Bed and Breakfast and she said yes. As a matter of fact, the Harmond's granddaughter is here this weekend and staying there."

"That wouldn't be Mrs. Brandon, would it?" I asked.

"Yes, that's her. We went to elementary school together and were good friends. But by the time we reached high school we didn't talk to one another anymore. Our families didn't hang out in the same circles. The Harmond's had invested in some profitable businesses and my family made a humble living selling flowers. I don't hold it against them, it's just how the times were," Stewart said.

"So, Mrs. Brandon actually owns Harmony Bed & Breakfast," Donovan clarified.

"Yes," Stewart said.

"Stewart." I touched his arm with my hand. Although he was no longer friendly with Mrs. Brandon, finding out someone you know has died is never easy. A lump of dread formed in my throat as the words came out. "Mrs. Brandon passed away late last night or early this morning."

He shook his head. "That's just terrible."

Donovan and I nodded in agreement.

"What will happen to Cora now?" Donovan asked.

"That will depend on Mrs. Brandon's son I guess. He will inherit everything now. How did she die?" Stewart asked.

"We're not sure," I said. "She was in bed and hopefully she went peacefully. We'll know more once the coroner does an autopsy and provides the actual cause of death."

The phone rang and Stewart excused himself to answer it giving me and Donovan a chance to process what we just learned.

I took a step closer to Donovan and kept my voice low. "So, I guess with Mrs. Brandon out of the way Billy has become a very wealthy man."

"It's a good motive for murder, if she was murdered," Donovan said.

"It is, but I still have a hard time believing a person could kill their parents, no matter how many times I see it on the news."

Stewart walked up to us holding the arrangement he had been designing when we came in. "I have to run next door to deliver this. Do you have any more questions?"

"I think we're good for now," I said. "Thank you so much for your time."

"Come back if you have any more questions or you want to buy some flowers," Stewart said as he walked us out.

A few doors down Dave's Deli had a procession of hungry customers lined up to the door waiting to order an early lunch. The special, a triple club with bacon and chips, was written in colorful marker on a board outside the entrance. I stopped and took a couple of photos of the sign and the front window with Dave's Deli written in white script.

Our next stop was Vintage Valor, an apparel shop. Circular racks of clothes, each with a chalkboard sign on top of the rack depicting the decade the clothes were from, covered the open floor plan. Strategically placed dresses and pants suites hung on the walls amid long strands of beaded necklaces, chunky purses, silky scarves, and hats.

A customer was being helped by a woman outfitted in a black dress with glittery fringe who looked like she was about to go to a speakeasy. A woman dressed in a blue nineteen forties skirt suit with a matching pillbox hat walked toward us with a smile on her red lips.

"May I help you?" she asked.

"Hi, I'm Kate and this is Donovan. I'm in town writing an article for *Travel in the USA* magazine and I was wondering if I could interview you."

"It's probably best if you talked to the owner, Ms. Belle. I'll go get her for you."

The dark haired lady's thick heels hammered the hardwood floors as she walked to the back of the shop to retrieve the owner. While we waited, Donovan and I browsed the merchandise. I stopped at the rack labeled nineteen sixties. I pulled a pastel and neon psychedelic baby doll dress off the rack and held it against my body, admiring my reflection in the mirror. It wasn't my style, but I liked it. I placed the dress back where I found it and was headed toward the register when I glanced to my right and saw Donovan on the opposite side of the boutique admiring his reflection as he tried on bowler hats.

Ms. Belle's poodle skirt swayed causing the crinoline to make a scratching noise as she walked toward us with quick, purposeful steps. She held out her hand and took a firm grip on mine. "I hear you're doing an article on Harmonyville, Georgia. How can I help?"

Donovan walked up as I began to ask Ms. Belle the same questions I had asked Stewart; how long have you lived here, how do you like the town, etc. When I was satisfied she was comfortable with me and my line of questioning, I turned my focus to the B & B. "Would you recommend Harmony Bed & Breakfast?"

"I would have, but after what I heard happened yesterday to Mindy and today to that old lady, no way. There could be spirits there," Ms. Belle said. She shook her head and waved her hand back and forth, slicing the air. "I don't stay where there could be spirits. No, uh huh. Cora's my friend and all but I just don't think I could recommend that place with a clear conscious. At least not until there was an exorcism performed; just to be sure there aren't any ghosts roaming around in there. But don't tell Cora I said that, especially since one of the ghosts could be her daughter, although I do hope nothing has happened to Mindy. That would just devastate her."

"How did you hear about Mindy and Mrs. Brandon?" Donovan asked.

"My brother is a deputy at the sheriff's office. Half the town already knows something happened over there. I overheard people talking at Trudy's this morning during breakfast."

"Trudy's?" I asked.

"Trudy's is a little house turned restaurant. It's outside of the circle, down the road a bit. A local's place," Ms. Belle said. "It would be best you didn't put anything in your article about people going missing or dying at Cora's place. She has enough to deal with; she doesn't need to worry about bad publicity too."

I nodded. I hadn't planned on mentioning anything about the deaths in my article.

"What do you know about what happened to Mindy? I heard one of the guests at Cora's saw the whole thing," Ms. Belle said.

"I...well..." I started. I was relieved when Donovan came to my rescue.

"We're not really sure what happened," Donovan said. "I know the police are doing a fine job looking into it though, especially with your brother on the force."

I almost laughed out loud at the line Donovan fed her, but she bit.

"Yes, he is great at what he does and he keeps me in the loop. Come back later and maybe I'll have more to tell you," Ms. Belle said. Her brow furred then she asked, "Is Cora's husband back yet?"

"No," I said, shaking my head. "Where has he been?"

"All over the east coast," Ms. Belle said. "He's a truck driver. He's normally gone a week at a time. When he has to go to the northeast he's gone a bit longer, but no one's seen him for six weeks. I think he up and left her but whenever I ask her about him she just says he's working. But don't tell her I said that, it'll upset her."

"So, you and Cora are close then?" Donovan asked.

"We are. I was at In Bloom Florist, a few doors down, and Fanny and Cora were talking to Stewart about something business related. I later found out they made a deal; she brings him roses from her garden and he sells her arrangements for half price. Anyway, as Cora and Fanny were leaving I complimented Fanny on her shoes and we all started talking and became fast friends."

"You've been very helpful, Ms. Belle, thank you," I said.

"Let me know if I can do anything else for you."

We left Vintage Valor and made brief stops in Bob's Barber Shop, Larry's Parts and Supplies, and Deep South Barbeque. The men in these establishments weren't as forthcoming with information about Harmony Bed & Breakfast and Cora's family as Stewart and Ms. Belle. They were more interested in fishing, building things, and the band playing at the festival tonight. It wasn't a total loss, though. The material they gave me would be the meat I needed to entice men to come to Harmonyville.

Donovan and I crossed the two lane street and stepped on the sidewalk in front of the next row of businesses. With a line of shops to go and only fifteen minutes until we had to meet Betts and Sid, we picked the one business we thought we would have the best chance of gathering local information; A Story to Tell: New and Used Books.

Large pane windows opened up the front of the bookstore and allowed passersby to get a clear view of the stock inside and the latest best seller propped on the display table. Lemon wood polish and ink on printed paper assaulted my nose when we stepped inside the narrow store. Decorative floor to ceiling cherry wood bookcases covered the interior walls. Vintage and first edition books were displayed on the top shelves and could only be accessed by an employee. Four square wood tables, with deep shelves on each side, were stacked with books and position in the center of the store creating three narrow aisles. A leather chair accompanied by a round table with a green desk lamp decorated the corner of the room opposite the entrance.

The only person in the bookstore wore a name tag and looked to be in her early twenties. Her long brown hair was pulled back in a braid with loose strands framing her face. I admired her beige chunky knit sweater. It looked similar to a piece I had at home, although I don't believe I could have pulled off her intentionally ripped at the knee jeans.

"Hi, I'm Susan. Can I help you find something?" she asked me.

"Hi, I'm Kate Westbrook and this is Donovan." I pivoted to the side to motion to Donovan, but his focus had been diverted to the "Local Authors" section of the bookstore. I looked back at Susan and continued, "I work for *Travel in the USA* magazine and I'm writing an article about your great town and the festival. I was wondering if I could ask you a few questions."

Donovan walked up with "A Complete History of Harmonyville, Georgia" hardcover book and a copy of *Travel in the USA*, folded opened up to the article I had written last month about Mobile, Alabama.

"Cool," Susan said. "Would it be okay if we took a picture together so I can hang it on the wall next to the article you write about Harmonyville?"

"Absolutely!" I felt honored someone asked to have their picture taken with me. I handed Donovan my phone and pushed my hair behind my ears, licked and rubbed my lips together to get the blood flowing and give them a little color. Susan and I posed in front of the leather chair.

Donovan and I took turns asking Susan questions about the small town. We were about to inquire about Harmony Bed & Breakfast when Cora walked in.

"Kate, Donovan." Cora nodded at us then turned her to Susan. "Hi, Susan, have you seen Mindy?"

"No ma'am," Susan said.

"Well, if you see her will you please ask her to call me right away?"

"Yes ma'am."

Cora left without saying good-bye.

"I hope Mindy's okay," Susan said.

"Are you friends with her?" I asked.

"Not really. I mean, we graduated from the same high school and had a few classes together last semester at Georgia Tech and I saw her at a couple of parties, but we didn't hang out together. The only time she really talks to me is when she wants something."

"What do you mean? What kind of things does she want?" My curiosity took over my tact.

"I don't know." Susan shrugged. "Stuff like wanting to know about guys I know and if I could loan her some money or give her answers to some homework. Stupid things like that." Susan became quiet, but I could tell by the wrinkled brow she was thinking about telling us something else.

"What is it, Susan?" I said.

"The other day Mindy called about something weird. She wanted to know if I had heard the rumor going around about her family."

"What rumor?" I couldn't stop myself.

"I really shouldn't say. I don't want something like this to end up in the article."

"I promise, I won't write anything about it. I am strictly writing about the town and the festival. I'm not even going to write about the death of Mrs. Brandon."

"So it's true, the old lady died?" Susan's asked.

"I'm afraid so," Donovan said.

"Tell us, Susan," I encouraged her. "What rumors are going around about Mindy's family?"

She paused and looked around the store as if she was searching for someone to rescue her. We waited patiently, with expressions of reassurance, for her to begin. "Mrs. Brandon and her family have lived here for decades. They're rich. I mean really rich. They own just about the whole town. Anyway, the rumor is Mrs. Brandon got pregnant and gave up her little girl for adoption and the word is Cora is the little girl. If that's true," Susan took a breath and wrapped her arms around her waist, "then Cora and Mindy stand to inherit a lot of money and half of this town." Susan rubbed her hands up and down her arms and kept her eyes on the floor.

I could tell talking about this was making her nervous. I needed to stop her before she became so uncomfortable she would be unwilling to answer future questions, if I needed to ask any more. "You've been a great help, Susan. Thank you for your time."

Donovan paid for his book and magazine and we left just in time to meet Betts and Sid on the corner. A group of little girls dressed in leotards with their hair in tight buns giggled as they ran past us and onto a small stage that had been set up in the corner of the park. A song I didn't recognize, but drew screams from the preteen crowd, boomed from the speakers. The little girls twisted and twirled in unison; as in unison as six year old girls can be.

When the dance was over I turned to Betts and Sid and asked, "How did it go?"

"Awe, man, we got the scoop." Sid bounced on the tips of his toes.

"Tell us over lunch, I'm starving," I said.

We turned back in the direction Donovan and I had come from and headed to Dave's Deli. As we passed A Story to Tell: New and Used Books I glanced in the window and saw Peter talking to Susan. I slowed down and watched them through the glass. Their exchange didn't last long and Peter started toward the door. I ran to catch up with my group before he saw me.

CHAPTER 8

The line at Dave's Deli had whittled down to half a dozen people, but the tables were still full. We stood single file with our necks craned at the four page menu stuck to the wall above the back counter.

Betts nudged my arm with her elbow and pointed to the back corner of the deli where four men had stood up from a table covered with crumpled napkins. Betts weaved around the close knit tables and to the back of the deli just as the men walked away.

Sid ordered for himself and Betts then Donovan and I took turns ordering our food. The triple-decker club with bacon sounded too good to resist. An overzealous girl with braces at the cash register gave us our cups and laminated numbers then directed us to the drink fountain. By the time the ice clanked to the bottom of my glass and the tea touched the rim, each one of our numbers was called.

Betts was wiping off the last of the crumbs when we arrived at the table. My mouth watered at the sight of crispy bacon poking out of the edges of my sandwich. I took a bite too big for my mouth and my cheek stuck out. I struggled to chew it to a respectable size. I pulled my notepad from my coat pocket and waited until I had taken a couple of gulps of tea to ask Betts and Sid what information they had gathered.

"Cora just found out Mrs. Brandon was her real mom!" Sid said.

"We don't know that for sure," Betts said.

"We heard something like that too," Donovan said.

I looked across the table at Betts. "Give me details." I adored Sid's enthusiasm, but I wanted the information given to me with a little less excitement. I didn't want the surrounding tables to hear what we were talking about.

"We went to the bait and tackle store and started asking questions, but the old man working there wasn't giving up any information. Not even about Harmonyville. However, his wife was listening to us and when he left to help a customer she came over and was more than willing to give us the scoop. She said Cora came in the library a week ago asking to see copies of fifty year old newspapers from Atlanta." Betts took a sip of her drink and continued. "She works at the library during the week and helps her husband at the store on the weekends. She said she would glance over Cora's shoulder while she was reading and it was all about Mrs. Brandon. She said there's a rumor going around that Mrs. Brandon was Cora's birth mom. I asked her if it was true she said she couldn't confirm or deny anything but she was smiling and nodding as she said it. She said it was the biggest story in town until Mindy went missing and Mrs. Brandon was found dead this morning."

"So, really it's still just hearsay," Donovan said.

"Seems like it could be bona fide," I said. "Rumors usually get blown out of proportion by the time they get all the way around town, but this one seems to be staying the same. Makes me think there's truth in it. If Cora really is the daughter of Mrs. Brandon, and she can prove it, then she could stand to inherit as much money and property as Billy does."

I shifted in my seat and felt something sharp poke my leg. I slid my hand into my pocket and wrapped the chain around my fingers. With care, I pulled mine and Donovan's earlier find out and kept it hidden in my palm. I leaned forward and hid my hand under the table until I was ready to reveal what I had to Betts and Sid.

"Of course, all this about Cora being Mrs. Brandon's daughter might not be true. What if Cora was looking up information on Mrs. Brandon because she's in a relationship with Billy?" I said.

"Like what kind of relationship?" Betts said.

"Well, maybe Cora and Billy aren't brother and sister but are something else, like maybe they're in a relationship," I said.

"Eww," Sid said. "Why would you even think that?"

"Because Donovan and I found this earlier today," I said, letting the locket slide out of my palm and onto the table.

"That's so pretty," Betts said.

"Open it," I said.

Betts pressed her thumb nails along the edge of the charm until it clicked open revealing the two photos inside. "That's Billy and Cora. Where did you get this?"

"We found it this morning when we were in the backyard. It was on the ground next to the bench leg. I was going to show it to you earlier, but then Billy found his mom and things got a little bit crazy."

"Whoa, wait a minute," Sid said, then lowered his voice. "You really think they're lovers? Isn't she married?"

"I don't know if they're lovers, but it's something to think about. We need to look at every angle," I said. "I never saw Mrs. Brandon anywhere other than on the couch, but Cora high tailed it to the bench when we went out to look for Mindy the morning she was attacked. What if Cora lost the necklace and didn't want us to find it when we were out there? That's why she went to the bench before the greenhouse, where I clearly stated I saw Mindy get attacked."

"Okay." Sid pushed his empty basket away from him. "Let's say Cora and Billy are secret lovers and Mrs. Brandon finds out and she gets all wild eyed on them because she's really Cora's and Billy's mom. Oh man, that's just gross." Sid sat back in his chair and crossed his arms in front of his chest.

"Oh, that's...I can't even believe...no, no," Betts said.

"Yeah," I said. "Let's maybe not think of it like that"

"You said look at every angle," Sid said.

"You're right, I did, but let's let the brother-sister affair be the very last conclusion we come to and only after all other possibilities have been exhausted," I said. "What I really want to know is who would want to, and have the opportunity to, kill Mrs. Brandon and why on earth are they trying to frame me?"

"That's a good question. Why would someone want to frame you?" Donovan said.

"Did you ever write an article that put

someone in a bad light?" Sid asked.

"No, I do travel pieces. My work is aimed to bring out the good in people and places. I think the killer is someone staying at the B & B. I honestly don't think Cora would kidnap or kill her own daughter so that knocks her out of the running with Mindy. Billy's a momma's boy. If she told him to hurt Mindy, I wouldn't put it past him. But," I said, shaking my head. "I couldn't see him laying a finger on his own mother. Mrs. Brandon has known Cora for a long time and they have built a relationship. I'm guessing during all the years Cora's worked at the B & B Mrs. Brandon figured out Cora was her daughter. She could have told Cora and that's the fight we walked in on. So that leaves us with Peter. Mysterious Peter. The man who never talks and always seems to show up out of nowhere. I don't know what to make of him. I'm still curious as to why he was in the backyard in the middle of the night."

"Maybe he's someone we should take a better look at," Donovan said.

"Do you think he has a motive?" Sid asked.

"I don't know," I said. "We know nothing about him, but I intend to find out."

"Don't do anything without one of us with you," Donovan said.

"I won't," I said to appease him, but I was touched that he cared enough to want me protected.

We sat around for fifteen minutes swapping stories and letting our food digest before walking back to the hotel with plans to meet in a few hours.

Back in my room, I sat at the desk and waited for my computer to come to life. I took my phone out and swiped through the photos I had taken earlier in the day. Along with the exterior deli photos, I captured several vantage points of the festival; the banner announcing the 10th Annual Fall Festival, autumn displays in front of the mom and pop shops, the band playing, and people from all backgrounds of life intermingling and enjoying the festivities.

I transferred the pictures to the computer then sat back in my chair and searched my brain for the opening sentence to my article. Sometimes when feeling stuck, I would make myself start typing words – anything to get my mind moving. I thought about doing that but instead, I let my eye wander above the desk and out the window to the rose bushes. In all my years I had never seen home grown roses as large and fragrant as the ones in that garden, which were still blooming despite it being October. I made a mental note to feature them in my article as one of the attractions at Harmony Bed & Breakfast.

There was a clear view of the greenhouse from my window. I pulled out my phone and stood in the exact same spot I was when Mindy was attacked and snapped a few more shots. It bugged me to no end that I couldn't figure out how Mindy and her assailant disappeared so quickly after the assault. There had to be a gap in the fence on the other side of the building or behind it or something because there's no other way to explain them vanishing.

I leaned against the frame of the window and folded my arms. I wondered if Mindy was completely knocked out when he hit her or if she was she still conscious. Did she know what was happening? Was she scared? Could she feel her body bump against the cold ground as he dragged her across the dying grass? The thought made me shiver and I sat back down at the desk.

I pulled up the internet and typed the word "greenhouse" in the search engine. Hundreds of images popped up. I scrolled through the photos in search of the same model conservatory as the one Cora had installed outside. It needed to have three walls of frosted glass, a solid back wall covered with siding, and a sturdy front door made of wood. Not one of the photos matched the design. I suppose the building could have been custom made or altered from its original form. That would explain why I wasn't finding it online. The words *give it up* scrolled through my mind like a ticker at the bottom of a television screen.

My thoughts went back to how the assailant disappeared with Mindy before I could get to them. The greenhouse had to play a role. There was only one of two ways to find out more about the greenhouse: ask Cora or go outside and get a better look at the structure. I wasn't about to go ask Cora.

As I stood up to get my coat, the blank page on my computer screen beckoned me to write, and I sat back down. My fingers moved in rapid succession over the keyboard causing red squiggly lines to pop up under misspelled words throughout the text.

Thirty minutes later, my first draft was complete. I turned off the computer and glanced out the window to make sure the backyard was clear of guests and Cora. Satisfied no one was out there; I grabbed my coat and left my room.

I was almost to the stairs when the sight of yellow crime scene tape in the form of an X across Mrs. Brandon's closed door stopped me. The answer to who killed Mrs. Brandon could be behind that door. If I could find some piece of evidence veering attention away from me and onto the real killer, I could clear my name. I had no idea what I was going to look for, but I had to try.

I glanced down the stairs to see if anyone was in the foyer then behind me to make sure I was alone. I wasn't by myself in the hall. A tawny, brown, and white furry body was perched in the corner next to my bedroom door. His bright green eyes watched my every move.

I had no idea how long Watson had been sitting there. By the intense stare he had fixed on me, I had a feeling he knew what I was about to do.

"What, it's not like I'm going to touch anything," I said to the Maine Coon. "I just want to look around."

Watson shifted on his front paws and leaned forward letting out a loud "meow." If he could talk I do believe he would tell on me.

I turned back around and slid my arm through the open space in the crime scene tape and wrapped my fingers around the door knob. I looked back at Watson who was still leering at me. For some reason, the cat watching me bothered me more than the fact I was trying to break into Mrs. Brandon's room. Not to be deterred by a feline, I twisted the knob less than an inch when the lock stopped me. I jiggled it a bit then let go when I heard footsteps coming from downstairs. I looked back at Watson whose accusatory glare was still fixed on me. I now understood how he got his name, the little spy.

I stopped halfway down the stairs when I saw Peter appear from the hallway and walk out the front door. He was so focused, he didn't acknowledge Goose, who came darting from the living room and across the vestibule in an effort to reach the threshold before the door completely closed. Goose was unsuccessful in his attempted escape, but it didn't seem to bother him too much because he ran back to the living room and perched his bottom on the window sill. His tail swished back and forth like windshield wipers during a thunderstorm.   Watson must have heard Goose try to get out, and then run back to the living room, because he dashed past me, knocking into my foot. I grabbed the banister to keep from stumbling down the steps. I ran my hand over my bruised thigh. It was around this time yesterday I took a spill coming off the stairs and Donovan helped me up. It seemed like so long ago.

I stepped into the living room where Watson had joined his brother on the window sill. Both tails swayed back and forth accompanied by alternating chirps from the cats' quivering mouths. Each step I took toward the felines was taken with care. I didn't want to scare away whatever was on the other side of the glass.

A quick laugh escaped me when I saw what the cats were looking at; a squirrel sitting on the arm of a rocking chair eating a nut, taunting the boys. The three animals stopped what they were doing when they heard my snicker and turned to me. Watson and Goose could have cut glass with the look they were giving me. The squirrel took a moment to assess the situation and decided his food was more important. He went back to nibbling his nut and the cats went back to stalking him.

I walked down the hall to the kitchen and

out the back door. Donovan's words rang loud in my head; d*on't do anything without one of us with you.* But really, how much trouble could I get into?

CHAPTER 9

The heat from the sun warmed my face as soon as I stepped off the covered patio. I veered to the left in the direction of the bench where I found the locket. I sat in the same spot as earlier in the day when Donovan was with me. If I didn't know any better, I would have sworn I could smell his Polo cologne. I twisted at the waist and looked behind me on the off chance he would be standing there. No such luck.

My hands gripped the edge of the bench and I leaned over, swinging my feet across the ground kicking up specks of dirt mixed with slivers of brown grass. With a feather's touch, I used my fingertips to brush the dirt off the toes of my suede boots.

"There must be something other than the locket out here otherwise why would Peter have come out here to look around in the middle of the night?" I said out loud to myself. Did Mrs. Brandon ask him to come out here and search for the locket? Was he nice enough to do that? He did give up his room for Billy. Or was that just a rouse to give him easier access to the backyard when no one was around?

I pushed myself off the bench and made my way to the greenhouse via the backside of the rose garden, along the fence line. My fingers bumped across the chilly Cape Cod style planks of the fence. I had hoped to find a loose board or two. That could explain how the culprit got away with Mindy so quickly. The fence was as sturdy as a house. Not one slat shifted in the ground.

Once I reached the outer wall of the greenhouse, next to the rose garden, I did a quick scan of the ground, kicking aside fallen leaves with my foot causing them to crumble. The only things out of place were strands of straw blown away from the base of the rose bushes where they were originally placed to keep the roots warm.

With care not to get pricked by thorns or break a stem, I moved the roses on the bush Mindy was standing above forward and back to get a better look at their petals to see if there were drops of blood on any of them. The fragrance was mesmerizing and I temporarily got lost in the moment.

A burst of cool air startled me and caused something nearby to rattle. At least I hoped it was something and not someone. The thought of being back here alone with a murderer made me hesitate and I thought twice about going behind the greenhouse. But I knew if I didn't continue my search now there might not be another opportunity. I mustered up the courage to continue.

Aside from needing a good bath to remove the thin layer of dirt covering the white siding, the back wall of the greenhouse looked to be in good condition. The span of the building was no more than five people wide and it only took me a few steps to reach the corner of the yard where the fence turned.

A narrow path, no more than three feet wide, ran along the side fence and the outer wall of the conservatory. One person could walk the passageway with comfort, but if two people tried to pass through at the same time their bodies would crowd one another. I couldn't imagine trying to drag a body through the walkway without a struggle, but I needed to check it out just in case I was wrong.

I bent over and took slow steps. I scanned every inch of the space. There were no divots, loose strands of hair or torn clothing caught on the fence. I was so fixated on the ground I almost ran into the shrub that blocked the exit. I didn't realize how big the leafy bush was until I stood up and saw it came up to my mid-thigh.

The branches spread out, touching the fence and the side of the building, making it impossible to walk around. There was no viable way of escape. If he had pulled her body over the shrub it would have caused serious damage to the limbs and leaves, all of which looked to be in perfect form.

I turned around and headed back down the path. When I rounded the corner of the greenhouse my face was met with another gust of wind and I heard another clatter of something nearby. This time I saw where the rattle was coming from. A piece of siding on the back of the building closest to the rose garden had a few missing screws and the ones that remained weren't completely twisted in their holes.

I got down on my knees and pulled gently on the loose section. The panel let out a moan as I nudged it away from the frame. I was able to pull the bottom half of the panel back enough to reveal a dark, seemingly empty space that was met with what looked like a piece of drywall. The cramped nook was only big enough to fit a few shovels and miscellaneous garden tools. It might even provide enough space for one person to fit in, but not two.

If Mindy was shoved in there she could have left something behind. I lay down on my side and pulled the siding back. I stuck my arm in the dark space and swiped my hand across the dirt. A hard object knocked against my thumb. I wiggled my fingers until I had a good grip on the item and slid it out from hiding.

My bottom grew cold as I sat on the ground and examined the long, red, dirt covered item in my palm. The heel was missing but I knew immediately this shoe belonged to Mindy.

I stood up and dusted the loose soil off my knees and rear end. Now that I had proof Mindy was back here, I needed to figure out what my next step would be. I could add it to my collection to take to the Sheriff or I could put it back and let the police find it.

Could this be what Peter was looking for in the middle of the night? If I didn't take it with me now, and this was what Peter was looking for, he could come back for it and then I would lose the only proof I had Mindy was back here. If the police found the shoe and dusted for fingerprints they would find mine along with others. Leaving it was no longer an option. One thing was for sure, I didn't need anyone seeing me standing in the backyard holding evidence.

The house was quiet and bare when I came outside, but that didn't mean it still was. How terrible would be if Cora or Billy saw me walk through the B & B carrying Mindy's broken shoe. I had to sneak it in without anyone seeing. The only place I could think to stuff the broken heel was inside my coat and under my arm.

Another rush of wind swept by me, this time

bringing with it the sweet scent of the roses. Unable to resist, I bent down and cupped a bloom in my hand and inhaled. When I straightened up, Mindy immediately came to mind. She was in this exact same spot smelling the roses when she was attacked. The thought made me feel uneasy and I turned around half expecting to see a shovel high above my head ready to come down on me with might. A breath of relief slipped out of me when I saw that I was still alone.

My foot had just stepped off the stone path that ran between the roses and onto the grass when I heard a man with a deep voice call my name. Sheriff Gathers stood on the back patio in a wide stance and pointed his thick finger at me. He jerked his head back motioning for me to join him.

"Hi, Sheriff, what can I do for you?" I asked.

"I have a few more questions."

Cora was sitting at the table with her fingers wrapped around an oversized mug of strong smelling coffee when the Sheriff and I entered the kitchen. She kept her eyes focused on the dark liquid inside the cup and let strands of unkempt blonde hairs hang in her face.

"Ms. Westbrook, we still haven't heard from Mindy," Sheriff Gathers said. He leaned against the island and folded his arms across his chest and crossed his legs at his ankles. "You were the last person to see her alive. Is there anything else you can tell me about the events leading up to the assault you witnessed?

I shook my head and kept my lips tight. I wanted to tell him about the bouquet of roses in my bedroom and the shoe I found out in the back of the shed, but not with Cora in the room.

"Okay then. You should know that the coroner has concluded Mrs. Brandon's death was not due to natural causes. With that said, forensics found strands of dark hair, about your color, in the scarf Mrs. Brandon had around her neck. I'll need some DNA so we can confirm it's your hair."

"Sheriff Gathers, someone must have broken into my room when I wasn't there and took my scarf, because there's no other way to explain how it ended up with Mrs. Brandon. Did they say how she died?" A lump formed in my throat.

"They are running some more tests to determine the actual cause of death before the final report is written up, but they know it wasn't due to asphyxiation. She was already dead when she was strangled."

"If she wasn't killed by strangulation then it doesn't matter she had my scarf," I said.

"Maybe, maybe not. Someone strangled her to either try to kill her, not knowing she was already dead, or to make sure she was dead. Regardless, it's your scarf, your hair, you're the main suspect."

One of the eager deputy's that had been at the B & B when they came to get Mrs. Brandon's body walked up behind Sheriff Gathers and aped the Sheriff's posture.

"Lots of questions Ms. Westbrook, lots of questions about these two cases and it looks like you're the only one who can answer them. You're the only one connected to both of them in some way," Sheriff Gathers said.

My palms began to sweat. I leaned over to

wipe my damp hands on my pants, shifting just enough for the shoe I had tucked under my arm to come loose and begin to fall. I caught it before it hit the ground, but it was too late. Everyone was looking at me. I stood frozen, the blood rushing out of my face.

The Sheriff took a few steps toward me and tilted his head. "Whatcha' got there?"

"I...um...I just found this outside, behind the greenhouse," I said, holding up the broken heel.

Cora let out a gasp and slammed her mug on the table. Dark liquid sloshed over the rim. "That's Mindy's shoe! We were out there yesterday and none of us saw it. How did you get that?" Cora buried her face in her hands and sobbed.

"It was hidden in the wall of the greenhouse. I can show you," I pleaded.

The Sheriff turned his head to the side and fixed his eyes on me while he instructed his deputy to get an evidence bag. The Sheriff pulled a set of handcuffs from his buckle. "Mrs. Westbrook, put your hands behind your back, you're under arrest for suspicion of murder."

CHAPTER 10

My hand shook as I dialed Olivia's number. While I waited for her to answer I assessed my surroundings. No phones were ringing, there were no scantily dressed women slouched in chairs, and there wasn't a belligerent man being wrestled into a cell by officers like I always see on television. What I did see were stacks of papers on every desk around me, a Most Wanted flyer on a peg board, and a thick officer sitting across from me watching my every move.

"Hello," Olivia said.

"Olivia, it's Kate."

"Hey, how are things going?"

"Not so good. I need your help."

"What's wrong?"

"I need you to call Harmony Bed & Breakfast and get in touch with Donovan as soon as we hang up. Tell him to come to the police station and bail me out of jail. Tell him I'll pay him back as soon as we get back to the B & B."

"What! You're in jail? Why? What happened? Are you okay?"

"No, I'm not okay. I'm being arrested for murder. They think I killed Mindy and Mrs. Brandon."

"Why do they think you killed them? Who's Mrs. Brandon?" Olivia said.

"In a nutshell, I was the last one to see

Mindy alive and I found her shoe outside and I had it when the Sheriff came to the house. Mrs. Brandon, one of the guests, was found dead in her bed this morning and my blue paisley scarf was wrapped around her neck." I pulled the receiver closer to my mouth and lowered my voice. "Olivia, I'm scared."

"I know, Kate. I'm so sorry. I can't believe this. Don't worry I'm going to get you out of there." Olivia's tone matched the severity of the situation.

"I wish I could talk to you about it more, but the police officer next to me is tapping his watch and signaling for me to hang up." If I hadn't been so scared I would have been annoyed with the officer's rudeness. Instead, I wanted to do everything I was told without question so I wouldn't get in anymore trouble. "We'll talk later, after Donovan gets me out of here. I'll call you."

"No you won't because I'm on my way there."

"No, don't come. I don't want Leo around all of this."

"Not a problem. He's spending the night at a friend's house and my dear husband decided to go on a weekend trip with his buddies. Don't worry, Kate, we're going to get through this. I'll see you soon."

After I hung up with Olivia, the rotund officer led me back to the dim holding cell. I was by no means at ease with the situation at hand, but knowing Olivia was coming to help me through this made my heart a little lighter.

Olivia and I had been through everything over the past two decades including breakups, college, moving into our first place, friend's betrayals, and so much more. Although, I have to say, neither one of us has ever been in a situation like this before.

The loud clank of the metal door shutting behind me stirred a disheveled woman who was curled up asleep on one of the benches. I walked to the other side of the holding cell, as far away from the woman as I could, and sat down with my back against the cool concrete wall. As much as I didn't want to believe this was happening, here I was, sitting in jail. I pulled my legs to my chest and hugged them as tight as I could. I laid my forehead on my knees and cried until my cheeks were soaked and my breath was labored.

Fear was hitting me like a boxer's gloves. Thought after thought assaulted my mind, each one deepening the tension in my stomach. Never once had I done anything that would get me arrested and now I was a suspect in not just one, but two murders. It could take years for an investigation. I could be locked up in a prison with murderers while they gathered information to put me on trial. I wouldn't survive in prison. I should have told the Sheriff everything when we were on the front porch. If he knew about the locket, the rose, the argument Donovan and I walked in on, and Peter snooping around in the dark the night Mindy disappeared he might not have jumped so fast to arrest me. I needed to talk to the Sheriff. He needed to know everything.

"Hey, who are you?" The woman sharing my cell asked. She sat up and rubbed a mascara stained eye with one hand and raked her fingers through a mop of short, black, greasy hair. She let out a deep, rattled cough that sounded like it hurt.

I wiped my face and lowered my legs to the

floor. "I'm Kate."

"Whatcha in for, Kate?"

"It's a misunderstanding. I didn't do anything."

"Yeah," the girl let out a laugh followed by a wet cough. "Me too, a misunderstanding. They got me in here for drinking and driving, but I wasn't drinking *while* I was driving." She found herself very amusing. When she stopped laughing she introduced herself. "I'm Cindy."

I tried to smile but the muscles in my face were heavy and I couldn't lift the corners of my mouth. Instead, I nodded in her direction.

"You here for the festival?" Cindy asked.

"Yes, and work."

"Where you stayin'?"

"At Harmony Bed & Breakfast," I answered.

"Cool. My friend's mom runs the place."

"Are you Fanny's daughter? Is the friend you're talking about Mindy?"

"Yeah, you know my mom and Mindy?"

"I met your mom at the festival and Mindy when I checked in. Have you see or heard from Mindy since yesterday?" I asked.

"No. We were supposed to hang out last night, but my boyfriend went psycho on me so I went to his place and partied. Why?"

"I'm sorry to tell you this, but Mindy was attacked yesterday."

Cindy stared at the floor for a minute then asked, "What happened?"

I told Cindy about what I had seen the morning before and then I went on to explain how Mindy was gone by the time I got outside.

"Huh," Cindy said. "So, you saw some guy attack her and then she magically disappeared?"

"Yes," I said.

"And you don't think she just got up and walked away?"

"No. I don't see how she could have. I assume she was unconscious because he was dragging her by her legs."

The edges of Cindy's mouth curled revealing cigarette stained teeth. "You know what they say about assuming. Look, she's probably fine. This is just the kind of typical, drama queen, need attention, stunt Mindy pulls. Last year she lied and told everyone she was pregnant by some married guy because she was mad at him because he broke it off, and so people would dote on her. I wouldn't worry too much about it. No body, no crime."

"Well, it's part of the reason I'm in here, so I have to worry about it. They think I had something to do with her disappearance or I know something about it. If you know where she is, or could be, I need to know so I can tell the police and get out of this place."

"I don't know where she is. Maybe she is dead."

Cindy's lack of compassion was disconcerting. "Don't you care?"

Cindy shrugged. "I guess she could be dead, I just don't believe it. Not with Mindy's past. You said it is part of the reason you're in here. What's the other reason you're in here?"

I stood up and began pacing the floor in front of the bench I had been sitting on. "If Mindy were faking her death, where would she go to hide?"

"You didn't answer my question."

"Tell me where you think Mindy is and I'll answer your question."

"I don't know," Cindy said. "Probably shacked up in some cabin with one of the men she's having an affair with."

"That's not a good answer."

"Hey, I told you earlier, I don't know where she is. Tell me why you're in here or I'll start asking people around town or better yet, I'll tell everyone I shared a cell with you and you told me...."

"Someone died at the B & B and they think I had something to do with it, okay."

Cindy laughed hard enough to throw herself into another coughing fit that shot the smell of stale beer into the air. Once she caught her breath she laid back down on the bench. "You're in deep. Good luck with that. Thanks for the laughs though. Now I need to get some rest before tonight's party. My head is killing me." Cindy flung her arm over her eyes. "Remember, no body, no crime."

Anger filled my veins and my pace picked up. Is Mindy faking her death? If so, why would she? It would be a bit extreme just to get attention. I thought back to when Mindy got hit on the head and I just couldn't bring myself to believe she staged the whole thing. I saw the shovel come down on her and her body fall to the ground like a marionette cut from her strings.

After about a mile of wearing down the floor, a lanky officer slid one of the many keys on his ring in the lock of the cage I was in and announced, "Westbrook, you're outta here."

Donovan stood with his hands in his

pockets at the front of the police station. We exchanged weak smiles and I tried to thank him for coming to get me, but the words cracked as they started to come out of my mouth. I stopped talking before another set of tears escaped my eyes. He placed his hand on the small of my back and walked me to his Cadillac SRX where Betts and Sid were waiting in the back seat.

We were a mile down the road before Donovan broke the silence. "I'm sorry I didn't get there sooner. I went out for a little while and when I got back these two," Donovan tossed his thumb in the direction of Sid and Betts, "ran up to me and told me you'd been arrested."

"It's okay. I'm glad you guys are here now."

"Me too," Donovan said.

"What reason did they give for arresting you?" Betts said.

"They think I had something to do with Mrs. Brandon's death, and because I was the last one to see Mindy alive. Of course the fact I had Mindy's shoe didn't help matters any," I said.

Donovan slowed the vehicle and pulled over onto the shoulder of the road. "What do you mean you had Mindy's shoe?" Donovan asked.

I turned to face the trio. "I went back outside to see if I could find anything to prove I wasn't making this up about Mindy and while I was out there I found her shoe. I tucked the broken heel under my coat and was walking back to the house when I saw the Sheriff on the patio."

"Why were you hiding the shoe?" Betts asked.

"I didn't want Cora to see me walk through

the house with it, and if Peter or Billy were guilty of attacking Mindy I didn't want either of them to know I had found evidence that could incriminate them, and then have one of them come after me."

"Yeah," Sid said, bobbing his head. "I could see that."

"Do you remember Fanny, from the festival?" I asked Donovan.

"She's pretty hard to forget," Donovan said.

"Her daughter was in the cell with me."

"Really?" Donavan said.

"What's going on at the B & B right now?" I asked.

"Cora's prepping for social hour," Sid said.

"Peter was coming in the front door as we were walking out," Donovan said. "His eyes were blood shot. Not sure if he had been drinking or crying, but when I said hi to him he gave me a quick nod and went to the kitchen. Of course, Billy was watching and listening to everything from the top of the stairs. When he saw me he snapped his fingers and turned around like he had forgotten something. Why was Fanny's daughter in jail?"

"Drunk driving. Is there somewhere we can go other than the B & B? I don't want to be around anyone else right now," I said.

"We could go to the Lakeside Golf Club," Sid said.

"Won't it be busy there?" I asked.

"No, it's pretty dead with the festival going on."

"Okay, that sounds good," I said and turned to face the front windshield.

"Kate, things are getting more serious by

the minute," Donovan said as he pulled back on the road. "We need to go to the Sheriff with all the evidence you've collected and let him take it from there."

"Yeah, I will. I want to keep searching for answers though. This is my life we're talking about. I'm not going to jail for a crime I didn't commit. I'm going to figure this out."

"I'll help," Sid said.

"Me too," Betts said.

"I'm in," Donovan said. "We just need to be careful."

"I know, we will be," I said.

The town faded behind us as we drove down the freshly paved two lane road. My eyes focused on the colorful trees that lined the pavement and miles of farm land with cows and horses grazing without a care in the world. I wanted to enjoy the beauty that was all around me, but all I could think about was what Cindy had said. Was it possible Mindy was alive and this was a ploy to get attention?

CHAPTER 11

We pulled into the parking lot of Lakeside Golf Club and I was relieved to see only a few cars there. Donovan chose the parking space closest to the stucco clubhouse and pulled in between the designated white lines.

The clubhouse sat perched high on a hill and required one to climb a generous, and somewhat intimidating, amount of steps to get to. To the left of the building was an eighteen-hole golf course. A large section of grass to our right separated the clubhouse and a row of boats tied to docks and secured inside boat houses. Layers of trees bursting with warm colors lined the far side of the lake. Three bolted down benches ran along the outer edges of the water and a covered picnic table was cemented down next to the last bench.

Aside from a young couple working together to tie their boat to the dock, the only other person I could see was an old man with his back to us throwing small pieces of bread into the water and on the grass for the birds to eat.

We passed by the three benches and sat at the picnic table.

"Okay, so Fanny's daughter, Cindy, is a friend of Mindy's. I asked her if she had seen or heard from Mindy and she went on to tell me about how she went to her boyfriend's and hasn't seen her." I proceeded to tell my group what Cindy had told me about Mindy pulling stunts to get attention. "The conversation with Cindy ended with her saying 'no body, no crime.'"

"Was she sober?" Sid asked.

"Yeah, I think so, but she still smelled like stale beer." Just thinking about her foul odor made me crinkle my nose.

"If Mindy faked her own kidnapping," Betts said, "then why hasn't she asked for ransom money?"

"I don't know," I said. "It didn't look like an act when I saw it happen."

Donovan rested his hand on my forearm for a moment. "We will figure this out."

"Thanks," I said. His warm touch sent sparks up my spine. I loved the feel of his skin against mine and the way his fingers wrapped around my wrist.

"Where exactly did you find Mindy's shoe?" Sid asked.

Donovan pulled his hand away and I turned my attention to Sid. I had given them a brief summary of events in the car, but now I went into detail.

"Why is all this happening?" Betts threw her hands up. "I just don't understand why all of this is coming down on you."

"I don't know either," I said, shaking my head. "But someone is trying to set me up so I take the blame for these crimes and I don't know who or why." I glanced to my right and saw the old man dump the remaining bread crumbs from his bag onto the grass in front of the bench he was sitting on. I had a feeling I knew him, but I couldn't place where I seen him before. It wasn't until he turned in my direction, giving me a full view of his face, that I realized who he was. "But I do know I'm going to dig and dig deep until I find out the truth, starting right now." I pulled my legs out from under the picnic table and broke into a slow jog. "I'll be right back," I yelled over my shoulder as I made my way to the old man.

"Where are you going?" Betts asked.

I didn't have time to answer Betts. The old man had gotten up and was walking to the parking lot. "Excuse me, sir," I said. He slowed his step, but kept moving. I decreased my pace to a walk as I neared him to keep from scaring him off.

"Can I help you?" he said.

"Hi, I'm Kate. I'm staying at Harmony Bed & Breakfast," I said, trying to catch my breath. "I saw you last night when I came back from the festival. You were with Mrs. Brandon and Cora."

He stopped just before stepping onto the gravel. He raised the bill of his hat to get a better look at me. "I'm sorry, I don't remember meeting you."

"We didn't actually meet. You were leaving when my friend and I were coming in and we didn't get a chance to introduce ourselves. I'm Kate Westbrook."

"It's a pleasure. I'm Jim Williams."

"It's nice to meet you, Mr. Williams."

"What can I do for you young lady?"

"When we were coming into the B & B I noticed you were having a rather heated conversation with Cora and Mrs. Brandon. I know it may seem strange, me asking you this when we don't know each other, but is everything all right?"

"It was a difficult night. I apologize if I was

rude to you and your friend."

"Not at all," I said, waving off the apology. "How do you know Mrs. Brandon?"

"I've known Betsy, Mrs. Brandon, for some time, since we were very young."

"Did you know Mindy?" I asked.

"No, no, but I was looking forward to getting to know her. I found out last night she is missing. Terrible, just terrible," he said, shaking his head.

"Yes, it is. I witnessed the attack."

"Oh, my, I wish you didn't have to see such a horrific crime committed."

He was sincere. Sorrow mixed with concern and kindness shined from his eyes and I dreaded having to be the one to notify him about Mrs. Brandon's death, but I felt I needed to. "I'm sorry to have to tell you this," I said and took in a breath of courage before continuing. "Mrs. Brandon passed away last night."

"Oh my goodness!" His hands started to tremble and his knees gave way enough to make him teeter for a moment.

"Why don't we go sit down, you look a little pale," I said, taking him by the arm. I placed him on the bench he had just left and sat down next to him.

"Are you okay Mr. Williams? Can I get you anything? Do you need some water?"

"No, I'm fine, thank you." He took off his cap and ran his age spotted fingers over his forehead. "She seemed fine last night when I left. She was just as full of fire as she was fifty years ago. I just can't believe she's gone."

"I'm sorry, Mr. Williams." It was the most

inopportune time, but I didn't know when another one would present itself. "Is it okay if I ask you something?"

"Yes," he said just above a whisper.

"Last night when my friend and I got back to the B & B we heard you and Cora and Mrs. Brandon arguing. I know it's none of my business, but did it have anything to do with Mindy?"

"No, no, it was about something Betsy did many years ago and I am just finding out about it now," he said. "We didn't talk long, just a few minutes before she told me something that has changed my life forever. I was so mad at her I could have strangled her."

His statement caught me by surprise. I didn't think he would actually kill her, but I knew if he went around saying things like that he would end up in the hot seat next to me. I needed to tell him how Mrs. Brandon died. "Mr. Williams, the police are saying Mrs. Brandon didn't die of natural causes."

He slowly turned his head to look at me. "How did she die?"

"Right now they're not a hundred percent sure, but they're working on finding out. They have to run some more tests."

"Oh my, why would someone want to, oh well, she is..."

"She is the what?" I asked.

"Nothing, it's nothing." He waved away my question.

"Mr. Williams, you can tell me."

His watery grey eyes stared into mine then gazed at the water. "She is mean hearted sometimes," he said. "I suppose I can tell you what happened. I'm sure the whole town knows anyway. Betsy and I went on a few dates is all, many, many years ago, and one of those dates went a bit far." He let out a heavy sigh.

I couldn't wait for Mr. Williams to reveal to me what I already assumed. "Mr. Williams, small towns are full of rumors and there's one going around that Cora and Mrs. Brandon are mother and daughter. Is that true?"

He spoke softly. "Yes, and I found out last night I am her father. How can someone keep the birth of your child a secret from you? What if I had wanted to raise her?" Mr. Williams turned to me. "I would have, you know. Then again, I guess that was part of her reasoning. She didn't want me and Gloria to have anything to do with her after all that happened. Yes, Cora and Betsy are mother and daughter and I am Cora's father and Mindy is my granddaughter."

"Gloria is your wife?"

"Yes, she was. I never wanted to go steady with Betsy, I mean Mrs. Brandon. I'm sorry. I'm not used to calling her anything but Betsy. Anyway, we only went out a couple times. She asked me out." Mr. Williams let out a quick laugh. "She was something. Women just didn't ask men out in those days, but she did and I liked her fearlessness, so I said yes. Gloria and I hadn't committed yet and I thought it was okay to casually see other women. I went out with both of them a couple more times and it was on my third date with Gloria I found out they were best friends. Gloria didn't know the other woman I had been on a couple dates with was Betsy. When she found out she gave me an ultimatum, her or Betsy. I told Gloria she was the one I wanted to be with for all my life and I would break it off with Betsy that night. That evening I went to Betsy's place and she got me sauced up on hard liquor. I was such a coward I needed a little liquid courage to tell her I couldn't be with her anymore. That woman had a way of refilling a glass without you being none the wiser. I was on my fourth drink when it occurred to me the glass was still full. Anyway, you know how situations like that can go. One thing led to another and now I find out I have a daughter, and a granddaughter, who's missing." He looked at the ground and rubbed his forehead. "I've told you too much. I'm sorry."

"No need to apologize, Mr. Williams. How did Mrs. Brandon take it when you told her you were going to stay with Gloria?"

"Whew." He leaned back as if the wind had blown him over. "That's when the real Betsy came out. Mean as a cobra. I had to take Gloria and get out of town. Who knows what that woman would have done?"

"Did you know Mrs. Brandon was here this weekend? Did she ask you to come back to Harmonyville?"

"No, my Gloria passed away a year ago this week. I came to visit her grave. I was going to head back to Helena where we've lived for the past fifty glorious years. Betsy must have known I would come to see Gloria because she showed up at the gravesite with her son, Billy. I was in no frame of mind to talk to her, so she asked me to meet her at Harmony Bed & Breakfast later that night, last night. She said she had something extremely important to tell me. Something that would change my life and it had to do with *that* night. I had an idea of what she meant, but I put it out of my mind until I was done talking to my Gloria. When I got there last night she told me about Cora and Mindy. I just didn't think it was possible for another human being to do something as cruel as to hide their child from them. Betsy proved me wrong."

"I'm sorry you had to find out this way and on the anniversary of your wife's passing."

"Yes, thank you. You know, I sure do hope Mindy is all right. I have decided to stay a bit longer, see if I can help find her and maybe get to know Cora a bit, or at least help her through this difficult time. It's the least I can do since I haven't been there for either of them all these years."

"That's not your fault," I said.

"No, but a parent wants to be there for their child regardless."

"How long has Cora known about you and Mrs. Brandon being her parents?"

"Not long. She said she received a letter saying her birth mom would meet her at the Bed and Breakfast at a certain hour and that's when Betsy and her son Billy arrived. I'm sure it was quite a shock for Cora to see her employer walk through the door and announce she was her mother – and that she has a brother. That was part of the argument last night." Mr. Williams took a deep breath of cool air. "You know, I am not feeling so well. I think I need to go back to my hotel and lie down."

"Do you need me to drive you?"

"No, I'll be all right. Just need to rest."

"Mr. Williams, thank you for talking to me. I hope to see you again soon with good news about Mindy."

"Me too," he said. I walked him to his

Chrysler and made sure he got in okay. Once he started the car and pulled away I gave him a wave then went to rejoin my group, who were now leaning against Donovan's car.

"Did you make any progress?" Donovan asked.

"He confirmed he's Cora's dad," I said. "That's what he and Cora were arguing about with Mrs. Brandon. Mrs. Brandon kept it secret from him all these years. Who does that?"

"A woman with evil in her veins," Betts said.

"Cora met with Mrs. Brandon a couple days ago and found out she was her mom, but didn't know about her dad until last night."

"Dang, that's cold," Sid said.

"So sad," Betts said.

"I think maybe now it's time to let the Sheriff in on everything we know."

"Do you want us to go with you?" Sid asked.

"Maybe, I don't know. I don't want you guys involved any more than you already are and I don't want the Sheriff to start looking at you three as suspects."

"I'll go with you," Donovan said as we climbed in his car.

"Okay," I said. We were barely out of the parking space and I was already thinking about how I was going to tell the Sheriff all I knew.

CHAPTER 12

Harmony Bed & Breakfast was so quiet I could hear the hum of the refrigerator from the front door. The peace was welcoming. We all needed a break from the morning's excitement. Donovan and I agreed to meet in the foyer around five to head to the police station, and then went our separate ways.

I rolled the beads on my necklace through my fingers as I paced around the queen size bed in my room. I couldn't stop thinking about what I was about to do.

Would it cause more harm than good to go to the police? Will I look even guiltier bringing in a pile of evidence that I have been keeping hidden all this time? He will want to know why I didn't bring the items in sooner. And how will the Sheriff react when I tell him I heard Cora arguing with Mrs. Brandon the night before she was killed, which makes her a good suspect? What about the fact that Cora's the only one who has a key to all the rooms. She could have easily slipped into Mrs. Brandon's room and killed her. Actually, I already knew how he would react to that statement. It was best to leave that one alone.

I could just walk into his office and matter-of-factly tell him where I found everything and go from there. But would I be prepared for the barrage of questions he throws at me or would I fumble my responses and look even culpable? I could put everything in an envelope and drop it off at the station when no one is looking.

Tired and a bit frustrated thinking about the Sheriff, I turned on my laptop and waited numbly for my computer to come to life. A photo I had taken of the festival from the top of the bridge leading into town filled my screen. I leaned in closer to get a better look.

A third of the banner could clearly be seen in the photo. It took me back to when I first arrived in Harmonyville, waiting at the traffic light, and watching the two young girls struggle to tie it to the trees. Seeing the gazebo brought back memories of me and Donovan sitting in the grass listening to the band. It felt like weeks ago when it had only been a day.

I wanted to stay in my daydream – continuing to block out the murder I had seen and the other one I was being accused of - but I had an article to write and a short period of time to write it. I would dream of Donovan later.

My cursor moved over the file containing the first draft of my Harmonyville article. I was about to open the document when something in the corner of the photo on the screen grabbed my attention. It was small and distant, but not so much so that I couldn't see the man was looking directly at me when I snapped the photo. I couldn't make out his face, but he was wearing a green jacket and a baseball cap.

I clicked on the start menu icon and pulled up my Pictures of Harmonyville, GA file. I chose the exact photo that was on my monitor and zoomed in on the figure. It was Peter, no doubt about it. What was he up to? Was he following me? I couldn't make up my mind which one made me more uncomfortable, Peter or Billy.

The article would have to wait. I needed to start eliminating suspects so when I went to the Sheriff I could present him with a neat little package of possible killers and viable motives. I shut my computer off and grabbed my coat.

Billy sat in the living room chair I had occupied the night before during the meet and greet. He stared out the window, absentmindedly petting Goose. Watson was sprawled out in the seat next to Billy, where Donovan had food snatched off his plate by a little paw.

"Hi, Billy," I said in a soft voice so I wouldn't startle him. Apparently I didn't speak loud enough because he didn't respond. I cleared my throat and spoke louder. "Watson, Goose, don't you boys look comfortable." Billy jerked his head in my direction. "Hi, Billy," I added.

He nodded, but didn't speak. Goose lazily lifted his neck and eyeballed me with half open lids then put his head back down. Watson yawned then jumped down and rubbed against my leg. "So, now you want to be friends," I said and ran my hand down the silky hair of his back. "Billy, I'm sorry to disturb you, but have you seen Peter?"

"Peter?" Billy looked at me with a crinkled face. "No." He shook his head and went back to peering out the window.

I gave Watson another rub behind his ears then made my way to the kitchen.

The aroma of baked apples and aftershave hit my nose when I entered the vacant room. Grey smoke snaked up toward the ceiling from a recently blown out apple pie scented candle on the center of the island. I did a quick scan of the backyard and patio. When I didn't see Peter out there, I turned to leave. I was making my way to the hall when Peter appeared from a tucked away corridor off the kitchen.

His face was clean shaven and he smelled fresh. If I wasn't mistaken, his eyes held the resemblance of joy. He started to smile when he saw me but quickly tucked his head and walked by me.

"Peter," I blurted out. "Wait, I need to ask you something."

"I have to go, can it wait?" His voice was calm.

"I'm sorry, but it can't. I need to know if you know anything about what happened to Mindy. Please, it's very important."

"No, I don't know anything. If I did I would have said something."

"But I saw you last night, outside in the dark looking around." I motioned to the windows. "And then today I saw you talking to Susan at the book store." He held up his hand to stop me from saying anything else.

"I'll explain later. Right now I have to go meet someone and it's very important. Later, I swear." Peter walked away before I could protest.

I balled my fists, shook them in the air, and let out a deep growl. The man was maddening. Not to be put off, I made sure Peter was gone and tip toed down the hall he had just come from where two doors stood open.

"Why hadn't I seen this yesterday?" I said out loud. "This must be the room Cora told Peter he could use when he gave up his room to Billy."

The door to my left opened to a white tiled bathroom with a matching yellow sink and toilet. A bright yellow throw rug with thin blue stripes finished off the sunny space.

To my right was Peter's room. I poked my head in. A single size bed pushed against a bare white wall with a short bedside table holding a lamp and a clock radio were the only pieces of furniture in the sparse space. Mustering up a little more bravery, I stepped through the door.

There were no windows and no closet. A few of Peter's shirts hung on a metal rod that had been anchored to the wall. His suitcase stood upright in the far corner of the room. The temptation to look inside it was too great to ignore.

I glanced behind me one more time to make sure I was still alone, then hurried to the corner of the room and squatted in front of the bag. I pushed the stray hairs that had fallen from my pony tail out of my face and laid the brown suitcase on the floor. The zipper slid open with ease. Would I just find a couple pair of pants and undershirts inside or something more exciting like Mindy's other shoe? I took my time lifting the top and was disappointed to only see socks and boxers occupying the piece of luggage. I zipped the bag back up and put it in its original position.

The room didn't give away any details about Peter. At least not the kind I was looking for. As far as I could tell, he was a minimalist who had a drab wardrobe. I let out a heavy sigh and twirled around on my toes to leave.

I was too shocked to take the first step. There it was, right in front of me. The wooden handle was worn, but the blade shone bright silver. My mouth hung open at the sight of a shovel propped up behind Peter's bedroom door.

I eased closer to the yard tool like it would bite me if I moved too fast. I knelt down and examined the blade's edge without touching it. A strand of blonde hair was stuck to the underside by what looked like a dark sticky substance. Could it be blood or skin from Mindy's scalp?

I stepped back and tried to calm my shaking hands and rapid heartbeat. Was I really standing in front of the murder weapon?

This was what I needed to give Sheriff Gathers to clear my name. He could test the handle and see Peter's fingerprints all over it. I reached out to grab the tool to take it with me, but thought better of it just before the tips of my fingers touched the wood handle. The last thing I needed was my fingerprints all over the murder weapon. It would be better, in all regards, if the police found it in Peter's room.

I didn't know where Peter went or when he would be back, but if he returned before the cops arrived he could easily get rid of the evidence. I took out my phone and snapped several pictures of the back of the shovel making sure I got an up close photo of the strands of hair. I angled the phone to capture all of the room, including Peter's suitcase and his hanging shirts. I didn't want there to be any question as to where I was when I found the shovel.

Once I finished documenting my surroundings I sped down the hall, slowing only once I had reached the foyer. I poked my head inside the living room to see if Billy was still there. He wasn't. I hoped he hadn't followed me to the kitchen without me knowing, but there was no time to worry about that. There were more pressing matters that needed to be addressed, like getting in to see the Sheriff.

I ran, okay, I walked faster than normal, up the stairs and into my room. I pulled the rose down from the top of the armoire. The edges of the petals had started to turn brown and were crisp. I wrapped a tissue around the bloom and placed it on the bed while I put the silver locket inside my purse. To be on the safe side I downloaded the new pictures I had just taken of Peter's room. I emailed them to myself and stepped back to take a breath.

Even though it wasn't quite five yet, I was sure Donovan wouldn't mind if I showed up a few minutes early, especially since I had breaking news to tell him.

I knocked on Donovan's door twice. When he didn't answer I decided a much needed walk outside would help release some of my nervous energy.

I went back to my room and put the rose back on top of the armoire and my purse in the nightstand drawer. I shoved my ID, keys, and phone in my pants pocket and went downstairs. My foot landed on the third to last step when I heard a deep voice that was becoming way too familiar echo through the foyer.

Sheriff Gathers stood in the living room with Donovan, Cora, and Billy. He looked in my direction and beckoned me with a nod of his head, again. "I have some news from the coroner. The bruises on Mrs. Brandon's neck were created after she died. Whoever killed her probably wanted to make sure she was really dead or did it out of anger. Either way, it was personal," Sheriff Gathers said.

"You already told us that. How did she die?" Billy asked.

The Sheriff adjusted his belt and stuck his thumbs in the belt loops. "It seems she was poisoned."

We all let out different degrees of gasps and waited to see if the Sheriff had anything to add. When he didn't provide us with more details I stepped up. "Do you know what she was poisoned with?"

"A flower. An oleander. We're not sure how it got in her system, but that's what the doc said she died from. She was killed by a flower." The Sheriff shook his head like he couldn't believe the words he was saying.

"There was a vase of oleanders by her bed," I said. "I remember seeing them next to her pill bottle and there were petals on the floor by the nightstand."

"Yes, thank you Mrs. Westbrook, we are well aware of that. Would you like to lead this investigation?" Sheriff Gathers said.

"No sir." A part of me wanted to slap the Sheriff, another part of me wanted to pull him aside and take him down the hall to Peter's room. "But I have something I think you need to look at."

"I'm sure you do, but right now I have others things to attend to."

"But Sheriff Gathers, it's really important," I said.

"What is it?" Cora asked.

"Oh…well…it's just…" *strands of your daughter's hair on a shovel in Peter's room.* "It's nothing, it can wait."

I nudged Donovan's arm and motioned for him to follow me. We discreetly stepped on to the front porch while Cora and Billy were hammering the Sheriff with questions. We sat down in the rocking chairs tucked in the curve of the porch. I kept my voice low and my eyes on the front door.

"There is a good chance the oleanders came from In Bloom Florist," I said.

"Yeah, I know."

"I think we should go talk to Stewart and ask him exactly how someone would poison someone else using those flowers."

"That's a good idea. You want to talk to the Sheriff before we go?"

"No. Not with Cora and Billy around. We can go later, when he's back at the police station." I let the air settle and Donovan relax before revealing my latest adventure. "I found something else, in Peter's room."

"Why were you in Peter's room?" Donovan's said with a mix of concern and aggravation.

"I snuck in after he left the house."

"What am I going to do with you, Kate?"

My mind went somewhere it shouldn't have and I had to quickly erase my smile. "I'm fine, really. Come with me to talk to Stewart."

"Now?"

"No better time than the present," I said.

We were almost to the bridge when we heard the roar of the Sheriff's cruiser coming down the street. With nowhere to hide, we turned our backs away from the road and faced one of the craftsman style homes, pointing at the trees like we had just seen something interesting. I didn't want the Sheriff to stop us for impromptu mini interrogation.

When the police car was out of site we continued downtown, but at a slower pace. It didn't seem to matter what circumstance I was in, when Donovan was around I was calmer, more at ease, maybe even a bit more confident.

"What did you find in Peter's room?" Donovan asked.

I scrolled through the pictures on my cell phone until I came to the ones of Peter's room and handed the phone to Donovan.

CHAPTER 13

"Look." I pointed at In Bloom Florist where Peter was exiting, holding a bouquet of white flowers. He took a right out of the store and headed down the sidewalk.

"Yeah," Donovan said.

"Those were the same flowers that were in Mrs. Brandon's room. Why does he have a bouquet of oleanders?" I thought about it for a moment then blurted out, "Maybe the ones he used to kill Mrs. Brandon aren't any good anymore and he needed a new batch of poison."

Donovan looked at me with a crooked grin. "I thought you said he killed Mindy. You think he murdered Mrs. Brandon too?"

"What's one more murder to add to his belt? Besides, I highly doubt there are two killers."

"Are you sure Peter's the killer? That's a pretty serious accusation."

"I know I'm being accused of the crimes. No, I'm not a hundred percent sure Peter is guilty, but I have a pretty good feeling he is. Oleanders and the shovel, that's way more evidence than my scarf, which, by the way, wasn't even the murder weapon," I said as I pushed through the florist's door.

The bell on the door rang out when we entered the flower shop. I loved the scent of cinnamon and I took a deep breath. Stewart was by the register working on another arrangement. This one included an ear of corn and a few miniature gourds.

"Hello!" Stewart stepped out from behind the counter wearing a big grin on his face.

"Hello, Stewart," Donovan and I said in unison.

"What can I do for you kids? Did you see something you liked this morning and have come back to get it?"

"Maybe," I said. I felt bad not buying anything and I immediately decided to return to the shop and make a small purchase before heading back to the B & B.

"Please, look around and let me know if you have any questions," Stewart said.

"Well, I do have one question," I said. I glanced at the glass shelves inside the refrigerators and then back to Stewart. "Right before we got here I saw a man walking out with a bouquet of oleanders, but I don't see any displayed in here. Do you have any left?"

"No, I'm afraid not. Those were a special order for Cora. The gentleman you saw leaving took what was left over from Cora's shipment. But," Stewart said brightly, "I could place an order for you if you would like."

"No, thank you," I said.

"They're poisonous, aren't they?" Donovan asked Stewart.

Way to jump in there, Donovan. In reality, I was glad I didn't have to be the one opening up Pandora's Box.

"Yes, very. Why do you ask?" Stewart said.

Donovan and I exchanged 'who's going to

be the bearer of bad news' looks. Donovan's raised eyebrows and slight nod signaled for me to go ahead. Unfortunately, I was getting used to being the bearer of bad news.

"Sheriff Gathers came by a few minutes ago and it turns out Mrs. Brandon was poisoned by an oleander flower," I said.

Stewart's mouth hung open. He looked like he wanted to say something, but his vocal chords wouldn't allow him. We gave him a moment to gather himself. "It was flowers from my shop that killed her? It is my fault she is dead?"

"Stewart, you didn't kill her, someone else did," Donovan said. "There's no way you could have known someone was going to use a flower from one of your arrangements to poison her."

"Who would do such a thing and why?" Stewart asked.

"We don't know, but we're trying to figure out," I said. "How could an oleander be used to kill someone?"

"Well, let's see," Stewart said. "There are a few ways. If she had honey made from bees that ingested the nectar that could do it. Eating the flower, stem, or the leaves could also be fatal. Although, why she would eat any part of the plant, I don't know. You know, if she had a heart condition or was ill, it would only take a small amount to cause her to pass away. A pinch or two in a cup of tea or sprinkled on a salad could be fatal, especially if left untreated."

"Did Cora say why she wanted those particular flowers?" I asked.

"She always orders them when Mrs. Brandon comes to town, they're her favorite. She always insists on staying in the oleander room with a fresh vase of oleander flowers by her bedside."

"The oleander room?" Donovan asked.

"Yes," Stewart said. "The wallpaper, it has little oleanders all over it."

I nodded in agreement even though I hadn't pay attention to the walls in room number one when I ran upstairs to see why Billy and Cora were screaming. My focus was on the bed where the lifeless body of Mrs. Brandon lay.

"What time do you close?" I asked Stewart.

"I'll be closing at nine tonight."

"Okay, I'll be back before then to pick out a nice arrangement to take home with me," I said, hoping to bring him back a little of the joy I had snatched away when I told him about the death of an old friend.

"That would be wonderful," Stewart said. "Do you have an idea of what you would like? I could make up something special for you."

"You already have," I said, pointing to all the arrangements displayed on the shelves. "I'm just going to get a little something from here to take back to Florida with me. Something in a vase or a pumpkin I can pull out every year that will remind me of you and your shop."

"You flatter an old man," Stewart said and went back to the flower arrangement he had been working on when we walked in.

I still had one more place I wanted to go before heading to the Sheriff's office with my evidence. Donovan didn't ask any questions. We walked side by side the short distance to our destination. I let my arms swing by my side; my hand bumped into Donovan's a couple of times. Even an accidental touch from him made my skin tingle with pleasure.

We turned the corner and passed by several businesses until we came to one we had become acquainted with earlier, A Story to Tell: New and Used Books.

This time the first thing I noticed when I walked in was the thin vase on the counter next to the register which held a single stem of white oleanders. I nudged Donovan with my elbow. My arm jerked a little too hard and jabbed him in the ribs. He let out a small grunt. Mortified, I threw my hand to my mouth. "I'm so sorry. Are you okay?"

"Yes, I'm good," Donovan said and smiled. I felt a little less embarrassed, but not by much.

"I wanted you to see the flower." I kept my voice low and pointed to the register.

"It's pretty isn't it," Susan said as she walked up beside us. "It's an oleander."

"Yes, it is pretty. Where did you get it?" I asked.

"A customer brought it in a few minutes ago. So, how can I help you?"

A skinny kid wearing dark glasses, baggy jeans, and a thin sweater walked through the door. He exchanged a mutual nod with Susan then headed for the thriller section. She turned back to us and smiled as she stuck her hands in her back pockets.

"Susan, I'm a bit curious about the man who brought you the flower," I said.

Donovan left us to go browse one of the tables where books were forty percent off. He was far enough away to make it look like he wasn't listening, but he looked up occasionally letting me know he could hear us.

"Why?" Susan asked.

"There's a man staying at Harmony Bed & Breakfast that I haven't really gotten a chance to know, the same man who brought you the flower. Anyway, he doesn't talk much and I was curious as to what kind of person he is. I can see by the fact he gave you a flower he has a kind spot in his heart for you," I said.

Susan picked up a stack of books that were on the checkout counter and started setting them up on the display table in the front window. "It's not my place to tell you about him. Why do you care anyway?"

"Because I think he can help me with a current situation I am in" I said.

"So, what do you want to know about him?"

"How do you know him?" I asked.

"I told you he's a customer," Susan's voice strained.

"A customer," I said, raising my eyebrows. "You must have made a great impression on him."

Susan whipped her head at me. "What does that mean?"

I shrugged. "He only got here yesterday and he's already visited you twice, once with flowers. He must really like you."

"How do you know that he's been here twice?"

"I saw him through the window after we left the last time we were here, and he didn't have flowers then. So he must have come back to bring them to you."

"It's not like that." Susan's voice intensified.

The skinny boy walked over to us with an open book in his hand. "You okay, Susan?"

"Yes, I'm okay." Susan placed her hand on his shoulder and gave a gentle squeeze. "I'll help you as soon as I'm done with these customers."

His eyes shifted between me and Donovan. I found his gesture sweet although I am sure it was meant to be intimidating.

Susan took a step closer to me and lowered her voice to a whisper. "Look, none of this is your business, okay. He's a friend of mine's dad, that's all."

"Your friend's dad is bringing you flowers," I said. Donovan casually made his way closer to us.

"No, you don't understand," Susan said, exasperated. "It's a long story, but the short of it is he hasn't seen his daughter in a long time and not for lack of trying. His ex-wife's a druggie and she snatched their daughter up one day and brought her to our town. She's just a kid, sixteen I think. She comes in here all the time with her boyfriend. He's the skinny kid over there. One day Peter comes in here and shows me a picture of his daughter and says he's looking for her. I tell him I know her and we get to talking. I told him I would help him set it up so they can meet without her mom finding out. I felt sorry for the guy and his daughter. They're supposed to get together this weekend. You have no idea how much he wants to see her. He's been looking for her for the past few years. The flower he gave me is being used as a sign to let her know he's here in town and the meeting is good to go. That's why her boyfriend comes in here every day – to see if the flower is here and then he will call her to let her know. Don't ruin this for them."

"I'm sorry, I didn't know," I said, feeling like a heel. "He never talks to anyone at the B & B and seems so evasive, it made me uneasy."

Donovan came over and wrapped his arm around my shoulder. "Kate, we should get going. It was good seeing you again, Susan." Donovan said, guiding me out the door.

"You too," Susan said and crossed her arms in front of her.

I glanced back through the window and saw the boy talking to Susan. "I can understand why Peter wanted to keep to himself. If I hadn't seen my daughter in years I wouldn't want to give away a secret meeting with her," I said. "But it still doesn't explain why he had the shovel in his room and why he was in the backyard in the middle of the night."

"No, but I am confident you will figure out the answer," Donovan said. He gently squeezed my arm before letting it go.

On the way back to the B & B we stopped off at Stewart's and I purchased a small Styrofoam pumpkin filled with yellow, red, and orange flowers and green embellishments.

Country music coming from the band in the gazebo echoed through downtown. They had drawn quite a crowd of Stetson wearing men and boot-wearing women. I saw Fanny from the corner of my eye. She was charming another man with her tight sweater and red lips.

The sun had started to set and the sky glowed orange. Donovan and I strolled back to the B & B. Only a few words were spoken, but there was no discomfort in the silence.

We were about to open the gate and head up the walkway when I spotted a navy blue minivan with a soccer ball air freshener hanging from the rear view mirror parked two spaces down from my car. I shoved my pumpkin into Donovan's arms and ran up the steps. I burst through the front door and rushed to the living room. Betts and Sid were curled up on the couch enjoying the heat from the fireplace. I was about to ask them if they had seen a red head come in when I heard a belly laugh accompanied by a few snorts coming from the hall.

"Olivia! You're here!" I yelled.

CHAPTER 14

"You're crushing me," Olivia said, laughing as I squeezed her in a tight hug.

"Sorry, I'm just so glad you're here," I said. "It has been one thing after another and..."

"Yeah, Cora has been telling me all about Harmonyville and the annual festival."

"She's been a pleasure to talk to," Cora said somberly.

As soon as Donovan walked in the door I grabbed his elbow and guided him over. "Donovan, this is my best friend, Olivia."

He shifted the pumpkin into the crook of his arm and shook Olivia's hand. "It's a pleasure to meet you."

"It's a pleasure to meet you, too," Olivia said.

Donovan walked by us and set my floral arrangement on the desk.

"Mr. Polo," I whispered to her.

"Approved," Olivia said, and grinned.

Betts and Sid joined us from the living room. I started to introduce the young couple to Olivia when I was informed by Sid they had already met.

"Well, now that we've all gotten acquainted with Olivia, I'll go get started on the hors d'oeuvres for social hour," Cora said, wiping her hands on her apron.

"Cora." Donovan moved to her side and wrapped his arm around her shoulder. "Let's skip social hour tonight. You have a lot on your mind and you need some rest." He glanced at me and Olivia, then over to Betts and Sid. "Why don't we go to the festival tonight?"

"I think that sounds like a good plan," I said.

"I'm in," Sid said.

"Yeah, we should go," Olivia said. "I need some fun."

"See Cora, we'll be fine," Donovan said.

"If you're sure...I don't mind fixing something for you to eat before you go."

"We're sure, Cora," I said.

Cora nodded and turned away. We waited quietly as she trudged up the stairs.

Once Cora was out of sight I grabbed my pumpkin arrangement and hooked my arm into Olivia's. "We're going up to my room to get freshened up," I said. "Why don't we all meet back here in thirty minutes?"

Half way up the steps Olivia leaned over and whispered, "He's gorgeous!"

"Shh," I said, giggling.

My room was about to become *our* room. Olivia dropped her overnight bag next to my suitcase and went to the window. "Is this where you were when you saw the man attack the girl?"

I stood behind the desk, which still allowed me a full view outside. "Yeah, she was over there." I pointed to the corner of the yard. "Did Cora give you details about Mrs. Brandon?"

"She told me she died, but no details."

Olivia pushed her thick auburn hair behind her shoulders and plopped on the corner of the bed. "So, what happened?"

I pulled off my shirt, getting a faint whiff of jail mixed with the outdoors. I took out a pair of dark blue stretch jeans, a blue and white stripe shirt, and a belted navy blue, knee length coat from the armoire.

"Where do I begin," I said, throwing the coat on the bed. As I changed, I went through every detail, including the conversation I had with my cell mate. After brushing my hair, I pulled out all the evidence I had collected and laid it out for her, then told her about the conversations I had with the shop owners. Had I not lived the past day and a half, I might not believe so much could happen in such a short period of time.

"Wow," Olivia said.

"Yeah, and the Sheriff doesn't know about the rose or the locket or some other things that could help my case, or maybe not help, but regardless he will be well informed before the night is over. Anyway, between my scarf, the shoe, and being the last one to see Mindy alive, the Sheriff thinks I'm the best suspect."

"Then we need to talk to the Sheriff as soon as possible and clear your name," Olivia said.

"Because it's just that easy," I said and let out a little laugh. "Here," I said, handing Olivia my phone I told her to scroll through the pictures while I finished getting ready. I let her in on my adventure into Peter's room when she reached the photos of the shovel.

"We need to get going," I said. "Donovan is going to the police station with me. So are you."

"Of course, I wouldn't miss it. Besides, I'm one of your alibis – you were on the phone with me when you saw Mindy murdered." Olivia said.

Olivia and I were the first ones downstairs, allowing us a few minutes to talk before the rest of the group arrived. Never one to complain about her job, teaching fifth graders, she mentioned some recent challenges with one of the student's inability to stop talking. There was no one better to meet that challenge than Olivia.

"Good, you wore a coat tonight," Donovan said as he joined us.

"Yes, this time I am prepared. Is everyone ready to go?" I asked.

"Who's driving?" Olivia asked.

Sid walked passed Olivia with his arm wrapped around Betts' waist. "We walk," Sid said, raising his arm in the air like he was leading his troops into battle.

We were on the downhill end of the bridge into town when Sid took a deep breath and let out a long exhale. "You smell that?" Sid said, licking his lips. "That is pure, artery clogging, delicious, greasy festival food."

Betts opted for a corn dog, the guys ate bratwurst and Olivia and I shared a plate of nachos smothered with cheese – hold the jalapenos. After our feast we meandered around the craft booths and talked about the best way to approach Sheriff Gathers.

"Donovan!" A high pitch voice rang out. "Yoo-hoo, Donovan." We all turned toward the sound. Two booths down from where we stood Fanny was leaning over her table and waving her hand in the air. Tonight she was dressed in a skin tight black shirt and furry white waist coat.

"Hi, Fanny." Donovan gave a short wave, then turned back to us. "Let's go over there." He nodded at the gazebo.

"Come here, Donovan. Don't make me come get you." Fanny let out a large laugh.

Sid gave Donovan a slight nudge. "Come on big fella, let's see what she wants."

We slowed our pace considerably and let the boys walk in front of us, giving us a better view of what was about to unfold.

Olivia leaned into me. "Who is that?" Olivia asked.

"An admirer of Donovan's," I said.

"Can't really blame her, can you," Olivia said and picked up the pace until she was beside Donovan. Not wanting to be left behind, Betts and I hurried to catch up.

Sid stood next to Donovan in front of the booth with his hands in his pockets and a huge grin on his face.

"Fanny, it's good to see you again," Donovan said.

Betts scooted next to Sid leaving me and Olivia on the opposite arm of Donovan.

Fanny glanced at me. "Oh, hi, umm…Kim, is it?"

"Kate. It's Kate."

"That's right." Fanny snapped her fingers. "Baby blue typewriter." She turned back to Donovan. "You see anything you like?" She leaned against the table showing off her ample bosom.

Donovan nodded. "You have a lovely

display...of antiques!"

Sid lowered his head and tried to cover his laughter with a cough. I attempted to disguise my laugh by clearing my throat and I ended up sounding like a camel.

"Do you need some water, honey?" Fanny asked me.

"No, thank you. I just had a tickle in my throat. It's gone now."

A familiar face strolled in the booth behind Fanny. She was wearing bell bottom jeans and a long tan coat with a scraggly fur trim.

"Ms. Belle," Donovan said. "It's good to see you again. Every era of clothing you wear from your shop fits you well."

"Thank you," Ms. Belle said.

"Watch my booth for a sec hon, I need to talk to Kim for minute," Fanny said and scooted around her table.

"Kate," I corrected her.

"Come with me." Fanny pulled me to a nearby tree. "I hear you were arrested today," Fanny said with a gleam in her eye.

"Yes, and I got the pleasure of sharing the cell with your daughter."

"Uh, yeah, that's what I wanted to talk to you about. She told me what you two discussed," Fanny said waving her finger back and forth. "Now, I'm not sure what is going on with Mindy, but Cindy is right, she's a liar, but sadly so is my Cindy. I just don't know what happened to those two. Cora and I are good mothers and to have such defiant...anyway, this situation with Mindy is serious and Cora is beside herself. I don't think it is some joke and I don't want it taken that way. Don't go spreading rumors about Mindy. I already had a talk with Cindy about what she said to you and…"

I held up my hand to stop her from continuing. "Fanny, I have no intention of spreading rumors. What I do want to do is figure out where Mindy is and who is framing me for Mrs. Brandon's murder."

Fanny pierced her lips and nodded. "You need to take a good look at who stood to gain the most from Mrs. Brandon's death. To be honest, the apple doesn't fall far from the tree. Mindy may not have suspected she was Mrs. Brandon's granddaughter until this past week, but she acted just like her from the minute she was born. They both had a way of making enemies. And that son of hers, Billy, he stands to inherit a lot from her death."

"You said they have enemies, any idea who they are?" I asked.

"No, could be a number of people. Look, I need to get back to my booth. Just be careful what you say to and ask people. This is a small town and rumors spread like chicken pox and I don't want a rash of gossip spreading about Cora or Mindy."

I held up my hands in surrender.

Fanny walked back to her booth sashaying her hips and giving Donovan a wink as she passed by him.

"You guys ready to go?" I asked. There was a collective nod and we strolled in the direction of the gazebo.

"What was that all about?" Olivia asked.

"She said Mindy and Mrs. Brandon had enemies," I said.

"Do you think she knows who the killer is?" Sid asked.

"I don't know," I said. "She said to focus on who would benefit from their deaths. The only people I can think of are Billy and Cora. But I can't rule out Peter."

"How are we going to figure this out?" Betts asked.

"Maybe we should search Mrs. Brandon's room for clues," I said.

"Kate," Donovan said, "that's a crime scene. You want to get thrown back in jail for messing with evidence?"

"No one will know," I said.

"How can we help?" Sid asked.

"You guys stay downstairs and keep a look out, like before. Donovan can stand by the door while Olivia and I go in, and let us know if anyone tries to come in the room."

"Is it wrong that I am a little excited about all of this?" Olivia said.

"Nah, I am too," Sid said.

CHAPTER 15

We opened the front door just in time to see Goose jump off the last step of the staircase and streak past our feet. He took a hard right and ran to the kitchen before we could shut the door.

"That is the craziest cat I have ever seen," I said.

"He's got personality," Betts said.

We started up the stairs and were no more than five steps up when Watson twisted away from us and disappeared into the upstairs hall. He didn't go far. He was sitting like and Egyptian statue in the corner next to my bedroom door. He had a great view of all the comings and goings upstairs. I assume that's why he chose that spot to perch.

I checked to make sure my phone was on silent and slid it back in my pocket. I could feel Watson's stare burning into my back. "We're going in," I said to Watson who replied with a heavy sigh.

"I know," Olivia said.

"Oh no," I said. "I was talking to the cat." I motioned to the corner of the hall where Watson had curled into a ball, his head facing forward. He pretended his eyes were too heavy to keep open, but I knew he was awake enough to keep tabs on us.

"Kate, that's a cat," Donovan said.

"It's okay, we have an understanding. Let's refocus. I don't know how much time we have. Okay, so, how are we going to get in the room? Do either of you have one of those metal things you slide in car windows to unlock the doors?"

"Why yes, of course," Olivia said. "I carry one with me wherever I go. It's in my purse, I'll go get it."

"Ha-ha," I said. "Very funny, you have a better idea?"

"Yes, I do," Olivia said. "I have a son that has a terrible habit of locking himself out of the house. We just need a screw driver."

"What are you going to do with a screwdriver?" I asked.

"Take the door knob off," Olivia said, like it was the most natural thing to do.

"That's a good idea except," Donovan said, "we would have a hard time explaining ourselves if Cora or Billy came walking up here and saw me holding a door knob, epically one that came from Mrs. Brandon's room."

"True," I said. I put my hands on my hips like it would help me think clearer.

"Has anyone tried to see if the door is unlocked," Olivia said. She reached out and wrapped her fingers around the brass knob and twisted.

"I tried to get in earlier and," I stopped talking when Olivia pushed the door open an inch. "Wait," I whispered and pulled her back. I raised my pointer finger to my lips. "Someone might be in there. It was locked earlier."

"When did you try to get in the room?" Donovan asked.

"A little while ago," I said. I ignored Donovan's pulsing, clenched jaw. "Olivia, knock on the door."

"Why me?"

"Because if Billy is in there he'll freak out if he sees me trying to get into his mom's room."

Donovan and I backed away and stood in front of the hall window. Watson lifted his head and slowly looked between me and Olivia.

After a couple of raps on the wood with no response, Olivia leaned over and glanced inside the room. "All clear," she whispered loudly.

Olivia removed one of the lines of yellow and black crime scene tape that created an X in front of the door and handed it to Donovan. We ducked under the other strip and entered Mrs. Brandon's room. I locked the door and flipped on the light, leaving Donovan out in the hall to stand guard. Olivia and I looked at each other with the same rumpled faces as the astringent smell of rotten eggs and Chanel perfume assaulted our noses.

The room didn't look much different than it had this morning with the exception of black fingerprint dust covering every hard surface. The sheets had been stripped from Mrs. Brandon's bed leaving the rose patterned mattress exposed. The image of Mrs. Brandon's limp arm hanging over the edge flashed in my head and Billy's loud cries echoed in my ears. A shiver coursed through my body like I had been hit with a blast of freezing water.

"You okay, Kate? You look a little pale."

"Yeah, I'm fine. You go through the dresser and I'll look through the nightstands."

"Okay, but let me know if you need to stop or leave."

"I'm fine, really," I said. "Let's hurry though."

The oleanders had started to sag and more petals had fallen from the stems. The pill bottle was gone along with the glass.

I hooked my fingers on the underside of the drawer, to avoid getting the fingerprint powder on my hands, and pulled. The severe smell of rotten milk struck me. Small curdles that looked like cottage cheese ran along the inside edge of the drawer next to the Bible, notepad, and pen. I had to cover my mouth to keep from throwing up.

"What is it?" Olivia asked.

I swallowed hard. "It's either cottage cheese or spilled milk. There's no cleaning that, that drawer needs to be thrown out."

"Disgusting," Olivia said, and then turned around to resume her search. She carefully lifted each folded piece of clothing and ran her hand over them, then replaced the item as she found it.

"Looks like you've done this before," I said, pointing to the shirt she had in her hand.

"Remember when Leo was little and he was always taking things and hiding them? One of his favorite spots was in his dresser, under and inside his folded clothes. I got tired of refolding them when I went on the hunt for whatever it was he had taken, so I learned how to search without messing up his clothes."

"Good thinking," I said. "Have you found anything yet?"

"No," Olivia jimmied the third drawer hard enough to shake the dresser and knock over the small bottle of Chanel that sat on top. She tried to grab it before it hit the dresser's surface, but she was too late and the glass lid fell off, allowing several drops of the perfume to trickle out. "It spilled!"

"How much spilled?" I asked.

"Just a little bit," Olivia said. She picked up the bottle and examined it from every angle. "That was close; I thought I had broken it."

"I wouldn't worry about it. It might actually make the room smell better. There's nothing in here. I'm going to look in Billy's nightstand." I glanced at Billy's bed as I walked over to his bedside table. It seemed odd to me that it was made up as if it had never been slept in. I highly doubted he knew how to envelope the pillow cases hotel style. That was more something Cora would know how to do.

"Olivia," I said. "Billy found his mom early this morning, right after breakfast. Sheriff Gathers asked me where I was between nine last night and seven this morning which means that's when Mrs. Brandon was killed. If that's the case, why didn't Billy notice his mom was dead when he got up this morning? He knew immediately something was wrong when he opened the door and saw her. It was pretty obvious she was dead. Her skin was all pasty looking. Wouldn't he have noticed that when he got up this morning?"

Olivia shrugged. "Maybe he wasn't paying attention or he got up super early, like five or six, and she was still alive."

"Or," I said, and lowered my voice meaningfully. "Maybe he didn't sleep in here last night."

"If that's the case, it's a shame. He could have stopped her from being killed."

"Unless he's the one who killed her," I said. We let the thought hang in the air for a moment before we continued to search in our designated areas.

A Bible and a few balled up papers were scattered inside the top drawer of Billy's nightstand. I began unfolding each scrap of paper and reading them. Scribbled in pencil was the time '7:45' and what I believed to be 'Lakeside Golf Club.' The other piece of paper had today's date and the word 'Harmony' written in almost indecipherable penmanship next to a doodle of a box. The last balled up scrap had been designated as a scratch pad to see how much life was left in a fading pen.

There was no indication if the time written down was morning or night, but I had a feeling it was when Billy was supposed to meet someone or do something at Lakeside Golf Club. With boats docked that could easily be untied and a vast lake surrounded by woods, it would be an ideal place to dump a body. I picked up the Bible and opened the good book to the page that was marked by a folded piece of notebook paper. Proverbs 1:19 was highlighted in yellow - *Such are the paths of all who go after ill-gotten gain; it takes away the life of those who get it.*

I unfolded the eight and a half by eleven inch piece of paper and began to read. My heart sped up and it felt like all the blood had drained from my face. "Olivia, I think I found something."

"What is it?" Olivia said, and came over and stood next to me.

"Read this verse," I said, and handed her the Bible. Olivia's eyes grew wide. "Now look at this." I handed her the piece of paper. I waited in silence while she read the list of names written with a black marker in impeccable penmanship.

"This is everyone staying here," Olivia said.

"Not only staying here, but living here too. Look," I said, pointing to each name as I read them out loud. "Mindy, Cora, and George. Actually, I'm not totally sure who George is, but I think it's Cora's husband. And look at this," I said, tapping the paper with my finger on the only name with a line through the center. "Betsy, as in Mrs. Bandon."

"Do you think it's like a hit list or something?"

"Well, I don't know about that." I let out an unconvincing laugh.

"Yeah, that is kind of silly, huh? Maybe it's just a roster of everyone here and Billy was keeping so he could remember everyone's name."

This time my laugh was convincing. "I highly doubt that. He's not here to make friends. Let's just say, hypothetically, it is a hit list, why isn't Mindy's name crossed off? And who wrote the names? The handwriting doesn't match the scrap paper I found in the drawer. It's too neat."

"Do you think Mindy is still alive?" Olivia asked.

"It's possible."

"This is freaking me out a little," Olivia said.

"I'm going to put all of this back like I found it and take pictures of everything, and then we need to get out of here."

I arranged the pages on the bed along with the Bible and took a few photos, making sure to get a clean shot of the handwriting. I crumpled up the pieces of paper and arranged them inside the nightstand. The Bible was last to go back in the drawer. I made sure the corner of the folded page stuck out of top. If what I had found in the Bible really was a hit list then we were all in danger.

"Can you think of anywhere else we need to look before we go?" Olivia asked. "What about the closet?"

"You check there, I'll check the bathroom."

The bathroom was a little smaller than mine. A medicine cabinet above a pedestal sink, a standing shower, and a toilet were all that fit in the space. I opened the mirrored cabinet to see if it contained any pill bottles or Mrs. Brandon's inhaler. A lowly pink toothbrush remained.

"Nothing?" Olivia asked when I came back in the room.

"No, let's get out of here," I said. I pulled the door open then quickly closed it when I heard Donovan's voice.

"Hey, Billy! What are you doing?" Donovan said so loud one would have thought Billy was hard of hearing.

"I need to get something out of my room," Billy said.

"Billy's coming," I whispered to Olivia.

"What do we do?"

We couldn't leave the room without him seeing us. The only option was to find a place to hide. My heart pounded against my chest. I put my ear against the door and listened to Donovan try to sway Billy from coming in. It didn't sound like he was going to be successful.

"You're not supposed to go in there. The police have it taped off, it's a crime scene," Donovan said.

Billy responded, but he spoke too soft for

me to hear.

"We have to hide. Now," I said.

I jumped back when I saw the doorknob wiggle. There was a pause, and then the key slid into the lock. Donovan said something else to Billy, which caused him to wait before entering the room.

"The bathroom," Olivia said.

I thought it sounded good until a vision of Billy pulling the shower curtain open and seeing two women huddled together in the corner played in my mind. "No, he might go in there. Hide under Billy's bed."

I let Olivia scoot underneath the box-spring first. I gave myself one last quick push under the bed just as Billy entered the room. We lay side by side on our stomachs with our feet beneath the headboard.

Donovan tried to enter behind him, but was blocked by Billy's arm. "What are you doing?" Billy asked.

"I was just coming in to talk to you. You know, see how you're holding up and all," Donovan said.

"I'm fine, you can go now." He closed the door in Donovan's face.

The quilt covering Billy's bed was two inches shy of reaching the floor. If he looked down at a certain angle there was no doubt he would be able to see us.

Billy stopped in front of the door and looked from the key in his hand to the door knob. It was then that I remembered the door was unlocked when we came in. Billy shrugged his shoulders, tossed the key on top of the dresser, and walked to the bathroom.

I waited for him to close the door to give us a chance to escape undetected. Unfortunately, he decided to relieve himself with the door wide open. Thankfully, Mrs. Brandon's bed impeded our view and we could only see his feet.

He left the bathroom without washing his hands and started across the room. Then, without warning, he abruptly stopped in front of the dresser.

"The spilled perfume," Olivia mouthed the words to me.

My pulse grew stronger. I had to slow my breathing so he wouldn't hear. Olivia's forehead wrinkled and fear radiated from her eyes. I shook my head like it was no big deal, but I knew it was.

Billy swiped two fingers over the damp spot and brought them to his nose. He scanned the room, twisting in all directions, and then wiped his moist fingers on his mom's bare mattress.

The springs moaned when he sat down on his bed, his feet mere inches from my hand. I pushed my arm tighter against my body. I looked at Olivia to make sure she was okay. She held her hand over her mouth to muffle the tiny whimper coming from her throat. Her body tensed against mine and I regretted bringing her in this mess with me. I should have come into the room alone.

Billy shuffled to the other side of the bed and opened the nightstand drawer. I propped up on my elbows just high enough to look over Olivia. I wanted to see what he was doing, but all I saw were the heels of his shoes.

The crunch of the scrap papers being unfolded was unmistakable. One of the slips of paper floated to the floor and landed under the bed. I held my breath. Billy knelt down and wrapped his fingers around the edge of the note, inches from Olivia's hip. He let his hand linger on the page. "Hello," Billy said, scooping up the paper.

Olivia's body froze solid against mine. Fear squeezed me like a snake killing its prey. Was he talking to us? Would he pull the quilt up and come face to face with us?

"I have it. Are you already there?" Billy said and stood up, moving to the other side of the room.

Our bodies deflated as Olivia and I let the air out of our lungs at the same time.

Billy paced in front of his mom's bed with his cell phone pushed against his ear. His other hand held the Bible and two wrinkled squares of paper.

"Yes, I can meet you," Billy said. He listened quietly to the person on the other end of the line then replied. "No, I haven't told anyone, especially not Gathers." Another pause. "Yes, I've done everything you asked. I'll see you then." He ended the call and stood still for a moment longer before turning out the light and walking out the door.

A drop of sweat slid down my forehead and into my eye. I stayed still for a minute longer to make sure Billy was gone for good. Olivia must have been thinking the same thing because she made no effort to get out from under the bed. It wasn't until we heard a small knock and Donovan call out my name that we slid out from our hiding place.

I cracked the door open and peeked out. The crime scene tape lay crumpled on the ground.

"Kate," Donovan whispered as he walked across the hall to his room. "Come on."

Watson was still in the corner and when he

saw us he dropped his head on his outstretched paws like he was relieved the tense situation was over.

Olivia and I snuck out of Mrs. Brandon's room and into Donovan's where Betts and Sid were sitting on the bed.

"I'm sorry," Donovan said. "I tried to stop him from going in, but I didn't want to force him to stay out and make him suspicious."

"We heard you," I said. "We hid under the bed."

"What did you find?" Sid asked.

"Notes shoved in the bedside drawer," I said. "One had the name of the lake on it and a time the other had today's date and Harmony written on it."

I looked at Betts and Sid. Behind the piercings and tattoos were two sweet kids. I hoped others would see them for who they are and not assume they were trouble just because they looked a little different.

I wanted to hold back the list of names I had found, but that may only cause more harm than good. If they were in danger then they needed to know and get somewhere they could be safe.

"What is it, Kate? You look confused," Sid said.

"There was a list of names," I said. "All of our names were on it, including Cora's, Mindy's, and I think Cora's husband. Mrs. Brandon's name was crossed off, but Mindy's wasn't."

"It was hidden in the Bible and Billy took it with him when he left," Olivia said.

"What do you think it means?" Donovan asked.

I dreaded saying the words. "It looks like it could be…it might be a list of people to…get rid of."

"You said all of our names were on it?" Betts asked.

Olivia sat next to Betts. "Don't worry. We're all going to stick together and nothing is going to happen to any of us."

Sid moved closer to Betts and took her hand in his. "We can go stay at my mom's if you want."

"Betts," I said. "I'm sorry for getting you into all of this."

"It's not your fault. You didn't make us do anything. We wanted to help," Betts said. She fixed her eyes on Sid's hand that was still wrapped around hers. She was in deep thought and we stayed quiet to allow her time to process what she was mulling over. "We can stay here," Betts said. "I have Sid with me and I know he'll protect me. And you have Olivia," Betts said to me, "but you're alone, Donovan. I don't think any of us should be alone."

"She's right," Olivia said. "Donovan, you will stay with me and Kate."

I opened my mouth to object and was met with Olivia's wide eyes and half smile.

"I'll be fine," Donovan said.

"This isn't up for debate," Olivia said. "It's already settled."

"We'll talk about it later," Donovan said. "Right now we need to go down to the police station."

"I'll go get the evidence from my room," I said.

"I'll go with you," Donovan said. "No more going off on your own. I mean it."

Donovan opened the door and led me out with his hand on my lower back. Watson had shifted back to his curled up position in the corner and was deep in sleep. I guess the excitement wore him out.

Donovan and I were about to walk in my room when we heard a woman's voice behind us.

"I haven't heard from Mindy," Cora said, shutting the door to her apartment. The apron she had on earlier was still tied around her waist and her eyes were red and swollen.

"I'm sorry, Cora," I said. "I know the police are doing everything they can to find her."

"We met a friend of yours when we were downtown, Ms. Belle from Vintage Valor," Donovan said. "She said her brother is a police officer and he keeps her up to date on what goes on in town. Maybe you could call her and see if he's let her know of any new developments."

Cora nodded and went back upstairs to her third floor apartment. I left my door open, with Donovan guarding it, and gathered the locket and rose. I double checked my phone to make sure it was still charged before leaving the bedroom.

"Betts, Sid, it would make me feel a little better if you two didn't come with us to see the Sheriff." I focused on Betts. "Maybe you could go to Sid's mom's house instead."

"What do you say?" Sid asked Betts. "Let's go to my mom's for tonight. We can meet them back here in the morning."

Betts' brown eyes met with each one of us and ended on Sid's. "Yeah, we can do that," she said with a sigh of relief.

"You have my cell. Call if you need any

help. I can leave Betts with mom and come back," Sid said to me.

"We will," I said. "You two stay safe."

Betts and Sid left at the same time Donovan, Olivia, and I piled into Donovan's car to go see the Sheriff. Panic flooded my body as I thought about what we were about to do. What if things don't go well? What if he throws me back in jail because of what I am bringing him? This meeting could turn out great and clear my name, or turn out awful and make me look even guiltier.

CHAPTER 16

The police station had picked up business since earlier this morning. A few of the previously empty chairs next to the desks now held an angry teenager vehemently denying his involvement in something to do with spray paint, an older man stared off into the distance while the deputy typed on his computer, and a woman who had had one too many drinks was hitting on the officer that had her handcuffed to the arm of the chair.

The three of us walked to the front desk where a middle age clerk with teased bangs kept her head down and focused on the form she was filling out. I greeted her and waited for her to acknowledge our presence. I was about to speak again when the phone rang. She looked up at us and smiled then answered the phone. When the call was over she went back to her form.

"Excuse me," I said.

She put her pen down and walked away.

"Excuse me!" I called out, annoyed.

She stopped and slowly turned around. Her nostrils flared and she cut her eyes at me. She was about to say something I am sure would not have been lady like when a young deputy walked up beside her.

"Hey," the deputy said, pointing at me. "You're the lady we arrested earlier for suspicion of murder. Did you come here to confess?" he said, trying to sound funny. I wasn't amused. The clerk, however, thought he was hilarious and let out an obnoxious laugh.

This time I was cut off from what I was about to say, which no doubt would have landed me back in jail, by Donovan. "We need to see Sheriff Gathers regarding the disappearance of Mindy and the death of Mrs. Brandon, please," Donovan said.

"Uh huh," the officer said. He kept his eyes on us and cocked his head to the side where the clerk stood next to him. "Carmen, go tell the Sheriff the lady we released this morning is back to see him. You three can sit over there and wait," he said, pointing to a row of wooden chairs that lined the wall.

We reluctantly sat on the hard surface of the seats. I took in a deep breath, inhaling wood polish and the faint smell of industrial cleaner. It wasn't that long ago I was sharing a jail cell with a kid who reeked of alcohol and stale cigarettes and now I was back here, just a few yards from the hall that led to the cold cement floors and metal bars of that cell. Before I could think more on the subject, and really have an anxiety attack, Carmen returned.

"Come on," Carmen growled through her crooked teeth.

She didn't wait for us before heading to the Sheriff's office. She had turned down the hall and was out of sight by the time we were half way through weaving around the sea of officer's desks scattered throughout the room. This, however, wasn't an issue. I knew where his office was. You had to pass it to get to the jail cells.

Carmen was waiting outside the Sheriff's office with a thick hand resting on a well-rounded hip. She had her head cocked to one side, and was tapping the toe of her thick, black shoes. "Well, come on. He ain't got all day."

We picked up our pace until we reached Sheriff Gathers' office. Carmen stomped off in a huff. The Sheriff waved us into the tiny room he called home at least eight hours of the day.

Certificates of recognition and a diploma hung lopsided on the wall. A single bookshelf was filled with books splayed out in all directions and stacked on top of one another. Papers and files covered the credenza next to the bookcase and the constable's coat hung on a rack that looked like it would break if one more item were placed on it. But the Sheriff's desk was impeccable. It held only the necessities: a phone, a stapler, a cup of pens, a note pad, and two manila folders. I glanced at the writing on the file tabs and saw Mindy's name on one and Mrs. Brandon's on the other – their case files.

"You ready to tell me what you know now?" the Sheriff said, beckoning me to sit down in one of two green chairs in front of his desk.

Olivia motioned for Donovan to take the other seat. She stepped back and leaned against the wall. Sheriff Gathers eyed Donovan and Olivia, but he didn't say anything.

"Sheriff," I said. "I have some items I think you will want. And they prove my innocence."

The Sheriff leaned back in his chair and cupped his hands behind his head, his elbows spread out like an eagles wings. "All right, show me what you have."

I stood and carefully laid each item on his desk. The rose was presented first, blood stain side up. The petal was brown around the edges, but the stain was still obvious. Next, I put down the locket, but not before opening it to expose the photos of Cora and Billy. Lastly, I laid down my phone, camera roll open and ready to scroll through, and then sat back down.

The Sheriff leaned forward and examined each of the items before him with his eyes and said, "Explain."

I stepped back up to his desk. "That is a rose petal that came from Cora's garden. It was in an arrangement that was put in my room after I checked in, and *after* I saw Mindy get hit on the head. I believe the dark spot close to the stem is blood." I pointed to the browned area.

"And you know this came from her garden?" the Sheriff asked.

"Yes," I said. The question itself put a grain of sand of doubt in my head, but then I remembered what Stewart said about Cora intentionally picking roses for my room. "Yes, it is and I would be willing to bet the spot on it is Mindy's blood."

Sheriff Gathers picked up the locket and held it closer to him. He looked up at me then back down at the open locket. His mouth twisted as he pondered what he was seeing.

"Yes," I said. "The pictures are of Cora and Billy. Do you want to know why their photos are in the same locket?" The Sheriff pierced his eyes at me. I took that as a yes. "Because they're brother and sister, the locket belonged to Mrs. Brandon."

"And how do you know that?" Sheriff Gathers asked.

"I did a little investigating on my own." That

statement made Donovan shift in his seat and I saw him cringe at my statement. He was right, I shouldn't have said that. I needed to continue before the Sheriff had a chance to respond. "I've talked to a few locals and the rumors about Mrs. Brandon are true. Cora was the little girl she gave up for adoption."

"These sources you gathered this information from," the Sheriff said as he let the necklace slip from his palm and back onto the desk, "they're reliable?"

"Yes, most definitely."

"I'm going to need their names," the Sheriff said.

"Mr. Williams," I said. "He's Cora's father. His wife was buried here last year. He will be in town for a little while longer before heading home."

Sheriff Gathers leaned back in his chair. "See, Ms. Westbrook, Cora and I have known each other a long time. We're good friends and I would know if something this important had come up, she would have told me."

"It all just happened, this week. Call her and ask," I said. I moved on to the next piece of evidence. "Then you have the shoe, which I did find outside. Did your guys check the flap behind the greenhouse, where I found it? Because I am thinking that's where Mindy's assailant hid with her after the assault and that's why we couldn't find her when we went back there."

Sheriff Gather's let out a deep exhale as he said my name, "Ms. Westbrook..."

Donovan rubbed his temples and said, "Sheriff Gathers, I know you want to catch whoever did this as much as we want Kate off the hook for

Mindy's disappearance and Mrs. Brandon's death. We discreetly asked some questions and did a little research. I ask that you please let Kate finish telling you all she has discovered. It's worth hearing."

I didn't think Donovan could get any sexier than he already was until that moment. "Thank you," I mouthed to Donovan.

Sheriff Gathers leered at Donovan for several seconds before he turned back to me. "All right, continue Mrs. Westbrook."

I pressed a button and brought my phone's screen back to life. My finger tapped on the photo icon and the pictures filled the screen. "These are photos I have taken over the past two days," I said, leaning over the desk holding my phone in front of the Sheriff's face. "This is a picture of the vase of roses in my bedroom." I slid past a few more screens until I reached the first photo of the shovel. "These were all taken in Peter's room." I pointed to his suitcase in the corner and then slide back to the first picture of the spade leaning against the wall behind the door. "I'm ninety-nine percent sure this is what was used on Mindy." I spread my fingers across the screen forming a v making the picture grow larger. "There's blonde hair and discoloration on the shovel base. And," I flipped the screen two more times, "these are pieces of scrap paper with Lakeside Golf Club, Harmony, today's date, and 7:45 written on them. I don't know what it means, but I think it's something worth looking into. I also found this list in Billy's nightstand."

"You were in the bedroom that was clearly taped off?" Sheriff Gathers asked.

"I, um…" I hadn't thought how to explain

that one. The truth was all I had. "I went in there to see if I could find anything that would help lead me to Mrs. Brandon's killer and whoever is trying to frame me for her murder. Billy went in there too, so if anything is missing you'll need to ask him."

"We'll get back to you interfering with a crime scene. Humor me and tell me what you've surmised from your investigation."

"It's Billy, Peter, or maybe Cora." I waited to see how the Sheriff would react to hearing Cora's name. When he didn't respond I continued. "Several of us saw Peter looking around in the backyard in the middle of the night with a flashlight the day Mindy disappeared. He also has, what I believe is Mindy's murder weapon. Billy stands to inherit a lot of property and money with his mom out of the picture. He would have to share it with Cora now that she can prove they're related, but if this list," I said, pointing to the picture on my phone, "is a 'hit list' then she won't be a problem for long. Mindy has already been taken care of. And then there's Cora. I can't see her hurting her daughter, so I can't explain how she could have anything to do with Mindy's disappearance, but I know she was angry with Mrs. Brandon and that could be motive."

"And what about the kids with the tattoos and piercings?" the Sheriff asked.

"They have alibis," I said. "They also had nothing to gain."

"So, what you're telling me is everyone at Cora's is a suspect except you two and the two kids," the Sheriff said, wagging his finger at me and Donovan. "And who are you?" He asked Olivia.

"I'm a friend of Kate's. I'm just here for

moral support."

"Uh huh," the Sheriff said. "Well, I can tell you now, Cora had nothing to do with her daughter's or Mrs. Brandon's death."

Donovan sat up, interested in the Sheriff's statement. "You've cleared Cora then?" Donovan asked.

"I don't need to. I know she didn't do it. But," the Sheriff said, "I wouldn't be doing my job if I didn't at least verify what you have told me."

"I don't believe she had anything to do with what happened to Mindy either," Donovan said, "but she has a motive for killing Mrs. Brandon."

The Sheriff's face turned red.

I needed to diffuse the situation before the Sheriff had a heart attack. "Sheriff, I have no motive to hurt anyone. I came here to write an article about your town, the festival, and Harmony Bed & Breakfast. But there are others with motives and now there is physical evidence. Peter has the murder weapon for goodness sake. Billy is an automatic millionaire. Cora, well I'll leave that to your discretion. There is one more thing. When I was in the jail cell there was a young girl in there with me."

"Cindy, bah, she's nothin' but trouble," the Sheriff said, leaning back in his chair.

"Well," I continued. "She seems to think that Mindy faked all of this and she's really alive and just wants to get attention."

The Sheriff stood with such force his chair hit the wall behind him. "I have had about enough. It's time for you to go."

I stood to gather the evidence I had brought in, but was quickly stopped by a large hand on top of mine. "All this stays here," Sheriff Gathers said with an eerily calm voice.

I wrapped my fingers around my phone and slid it off the desk. I would email him the photos, but I needed my phone. I cupped the phone in my hand and held it close to my body. I followed Olivia and Donovan out of the Sheriff's office without saying another word.

We rushed through the police station and were just on the other side of the reception area, with Carmen eyeballing us, when the Sheriff's voice bellowed my name from across the room.

I turned and saw him in the hall doorway with his hands on his hips. The blood rushed from my face. He must have seen me swipe my phone. I held my breath and waited.

"I'll be in touch Mrs. Westbrook. I'll be by in the morning. Don't leave town."

I nodded and hurried out the front door and into the cool air. I filled my lungs with oxygen and jumped into the front seat of Donovan's SUV.

"I'm not sure that went so well," Olivia said as she got in the backseat.

"Maybe not, but the seed has been planted," I said. "Whether he wants to or not, he'll think about what I said. The only thing is I don't know how quickly he'll act. If he doesn't move fast enough there might be another name crossed off that list."

CHAPTER 17

After the day I had, I was ready for a nice, smooth glass of wine. I called Sid once Donovan and I were on the road and asked him where I could get a drink without having to hear town gossip.

"Sid said he and Betts will meet us at Lakeside Golf Club," I said.

Betts and Sid were standing at the entrance of the clubhouse when we pulled into the parking lot.

Thirty-two steps. That's how many I counted as I trudged up the hill. I inhaled a gulp of cool air in an attempt to catch my breath when we reached the top of the steps, then followed my group into the lobby. I stopped a few feet into the room and let myself adjust to the ambiance of the space.

I felt like I was in a time warp. The nineteen seventies red, orange, and yellow wave pattern in the carpet made me dizzy. A single window, facing the lake, was flanked by a couple of yellow gold high-back chairs separated by a small round table and a flower arrangement of fake roses, not the silky kind. The wood panel reception desk, to the left of the entrance, was topped with a gold lamp and a telephone. A few faded posters bragged about this being the "Best Golf Course in Georgia." I imagine at one time this place could have been called the best, but that time had long gone.

To the right of the welcome desk stood a sign atop a brass stand informing us we could turn left and go down the hall to use the restroom or shop at the gift store, however, if we continued straight ahead, we would enter the bar and lounge. We opted to go straight.

Donovan held the glass door to the lounge open and we entered the bar single file. The bartender, dressed in a silk flower button up shirt with an oversized collar, greeted us with a smile and a nod. Between his attire, the paneled walls, and the orange leather chairs pushed under the dining tables, I came to the assumption the decor was intentional and not original to the building.

The far wall held a wide stone fireplace with brown couches flanking each side. Two men sat across from one another holding glasses of dark liquid on the rocks. A couple of seasoned men clad in white pants and Panama hats with grey hairs poking out from underneath the brim were finishing off their dinner at one of the tables next to the exterior wall which was constructed of floor to ceiling windows.

Betts, Olivia, and I gave the guys our drink order and plopped down in the fake leather seats at one of the tables next to the windows. My arms lay limp on the armrests as I stared outside. My energy was waning. I watched tiny ripples on the water created by the wind, sparkle from the light of the moon and nearby boathouses.

Sid handed Betts a bottle of beer and sat down. Donovan passed me and Olivia our glasses of Pinot Noir then went back to the bar to grab his drink before joining us.

There was a silence in the room

uncharacteristic of a bar and lounge. Aside from the crackle coming from the fireplace and soft instrumental music emanating from the overhead speakers, as well as the occasional bout of laughter from one of the men, it was so quiet I felt like I was in a library.

To be honest, I was grateful for the peace and quiet. The day was winding down and so was I. The saggy eyes and somber faces at my table let me know I wasn't the only one feeling this way. I took a sip of my wine and let the smooth red liquid glide down my throat.

We kept our conversations light and focused a variety of subjects, Harmonyville, Georgia not being one of them. Sid told us about his studies in biology and Betts pulled out her phone and showed us pictures of her metal sculptures. Olivia regaled the group with a story about our one and only camping trip that took place ten years ago, right before she became pregnant with Leo. We snuck a canoe out onto the lake and about a hundred yards into our mission I lost one of the oars and thought it would be a good idea to stand up in the boat and wave frantically to the family on the shore for help. Moments after my bright idea, we tipped over and had to swim back to land, leaving the boat to bob in the water until it could be rescued.

The reminiscence brought on a much needed laugh. With everything that had gone on this weekend, this was the one moment I wanted to burn in my mind and pull up years from now when I looked back at my time in Harmonyville, Georgia.

The tension I carried in my shoulders from these past two days had started to release its grip. I leaned back in my chair and glanced out the window at the lake. A light from one of the boathouses turned on and I saw a tall, thin man in a green coat and baseball cap open the door and step out. He reached above his head and clicked a padlock in place and put the key in his coat pocket. He walked the perimeter of the building with his head cast down. I put my glass on the table and studied his movements.

"What is it, Kate?" Donovan asked.

"That man out there by the boathouse," I said, pointing to the only person I could see outside.

"What about him?" Donovan asked.

"He just locked the door from the outside and now he's walking around the building like he's looking for something. He kind of reminds me of Peter last night in the backyard," I said.

"Relax, Kate," Olivia said. "What are the odds that Peter is out there doing the exact same thing he did last night, especially since you called him out earlier today in the kitchen when you told him you saw him lurking around in the dark. Listen, this is what you're going to do. You're going to drink wine until you're to pass out and then we're going to take you back to the Bed and Breakfast and you're going to get a good night's sleep. We'll worry about everything else in the morning when you're fully rested."

I nodded then turned my attention back to the man who was still roaming around the boathouse. "What if that's him? What if it's Peter and Mindy's body is in the boathouse?" I said.

"If it is Peter we need to leave him alone," Donovan said. "Remember what Susan, from the bookstore said, he's supposed to meet his daughter tonight. Maybe this is where they're meeting."

"Maybe." I swallowed the last sip of wine in my glass and stood up too fast. I placed my fingertips on the table to balance myself. "But there's only one way to find out."

"Wait, Kate," Donovan said. "Let's just watch him for a minute and see what happens."

"Kate," Sid said. "Maybe you should sit down."

I shook my head in an attempt to disagree with Sid, but instead I started to lose my footing and the room began to sway. I closed my eyes to try to stop the vertigo, but it only made it worse. I sat back down.

"Maybe you don't need any more wine," Olivia said.

"I'm fine" I said. "I want to get a look inside the boathouse. Something about this isn't sitting right with me."

"Uh, that would be the wine," Sid said.

"We need to get some food in you," Donovan said.

"No, I'm fine, really. I just stood up too fast." I looked back out the window and watched the man walk away from the boathouse and head in the direction of the parking lot. "But some fresh air might do me good." I pushed my chair back and hurried to the door of the lounge.

"Wait up," Olivia said. She caught up to me as I exited the bar.

"Ladies," I heard Donovan yell out as the glass door to the lounge shut behind us. We ran down the short hall and into the lobby where we were abruptly stopped by a woman with a bun wrapped so tight on top of her head it tugged at the sides of her face making her look like she had a botched facelift.

"*Do not* run through this building," she said, tugging on the bottom of her black skirt suit jacket.

Olivia and I froze. I thought back to high school and the only time Olivia and I tried, and failed, to skip a class. "Um," *focus Kate.* "We need to get outside, before our friend leaves," I said.

The woman sneered at us and folded her arms across her chest.

Olivia said, "He was waiting for us outside and we were waiting for him inside." Olivia let out a short laugh. "We really can't miss him. We won't run, we promise."

The woman stepped to the side of us and watched Betts, Sid, and Donovan as they entered the lobby from the lounge. Olivia and I took the opportunity to slide past the hall monitor and dash outside.

The cold air struck me and cleared my head. We stood at the top of the stairs and watched the man in the green coat and baseball hat drive away. The rear lights of his car lit up as he stopped to look for oncoming traffic and then turn left out of the parking lot.

"Was it him?" Sid asked as he walked up behind us with Donovan and Betts by his side.

Olivia shook her head. "Don't know. He was leaving the parking lot when we got out here."

I glanced over at the boathouse he emerged from then back at the road. His taillights had faded out of sight and the street was dark again. I looked back to the boathouse. A sliver of a window near the roof line of the building was illuminated by the exterior light. If I could figure out a way to reach the window I would be able to see inside.

"Kate," Donovan said, touching my arm. "What are you thinking about?"

"I'm going to check out the boathouse," I said.

"Do you think that's a good idea?" Olivia said. "What if he comes back or someone inside the restaurant sees us and tells him we were looking around?"

"I think it's a good idea," Sid said.

"Of course you do," Betts said, exhaling hard enough we could see her breath.

The five of us shuffled down the grassy hill. It was the fastest, and most fun, way to get to our destination. We made it to the boathouse without any of us falling down, which in my current state was a miracle.

"Look," I said and pointed up at the window near the metal roof. A small storage shed made of the same wood as the boathouse sat directly below the window. "If you help me up on the shed," I said to Donovan, "I think I'll be able to look inside."

Donovan wrapped his hands around my waist and hoisted me up on the flat surface. I stood on the tips of my toes in an effort to look through the window, but I was a few inches too short.

"Get up here with me and put me on your shoulders," I said to Donovan. Olivia's eyes and mouth grew wide. To speak to a man so brazenly wasn't my style, but with a little help from my friend Pinot Noir and a possible murder charge hanging over my head, all inhibition was pushed aside. From the smile on Donovan's face, I believe he didn't mind it so much.

Donovan hopped up on the shed and knelt down. I wrapped my legs around his neck and with a slow ascent he lifted me up. His hands held on to my thighs to keep me steady. This time the fog of breath billowed from my mouth when I let out a deep exhale. *Focus Kate.*

I wrapped my fingers around the window sill and craned my neck. The moon gave off enough of a glow to see inside. A speed boat hung from chains above the water, fishing gear was mounted on the wall, and a crumpled blanket with piece of rope next to it lay on the floor next to a vase filled with oleanders.

"Okay, you can let me down," I said.

Donovan slowly lowered my feet to the ground and we stood facing each other, only inches apart. "There's a vase of oleanders, a blanket, and some rope," I whispered.

"Don't jump to conclusions. Peter bought the flowers for his daughter and it is cold outside and there's always rope where a boat's involved," Donovan said.

His body was so close to mine all I had to do was pretend to lose my balance and fall into him causing our lips to touch. As tempting as that was, and the temptation was strong, I didn't want our first kiss to happen that way. But if I didn't move away from him fast, that's exactly how our first kiss would take place. I squatted down and jumped off the shed.

"What did you see?" Olivia asked me.

I repeated what I had just told Donovan.

"No body?" Olivia asked.

"No body," I said.

"Hey, guys," Betts said, pointing at the set of stairs in front of the clubhouse.

The tight faced woman in the skirt suit stomped down each step. "Hey! You!" The lady pointed at us with a stiff arm.

Without hesitation we all took off running down the edge of the lake and to the parking lot. Donovan clicked a button to release the locks of his SUV. I jumped in the front seat and Olivia hurried to the backseat. Betts and Sid made it to their car a few spaces down just the red faced woman arrived at Donovan's door.

"What were you doing out there?" The woman demanded. She pulled on the handle of the driver's side door in an attempt to open it, but Donovan had already set the locks. "Who are you? What do you want? I'm calling the police!"

Donovan nodded and put the car in reverse. He slowly backed up to keep from hitting the irate woman, and then put the vehicle in drive. I turned around in my seat and watched the woman march back to the building with clenched fists.

"That was close and a little bit scary," Olivia said.

"Too close," I said. I closed my eyes and let the sound of the tires rolling against the pavement calm me. "What time is it?"

"A little after eight," Donovan said.

"It feels like midnight," I said.

"Wait a minute," Olivia said, leaning forward between the driver and passenger seats.

"What?" I asked and let my head roll to the side to face her.

"Didn't the piece of paper you found in Billy's drawer have seven forty five written on it?"

"Yes, it did," I said. I sat up straight in my seat. "What if that wasn't Peter, but Billy out there and he was meeting whoever he was on the phone with earlier?"

"But he left without meeting anyone," Donovan said.

"That we saw. Maybe there was someone in the boathouse and they got out before we got down there," I said. "Sheriff Gathers needs to come out here and check on this. Let's go back to the station."

"We can go in the morning and tell him about the boathouse and see if he's found out any new information pertaining to what you brought in," Donovan said. "There's nothing else we can do tonight and worrying about it won't change it. Besides, if he smells alcohol on your breath there's no telling what he'll do."

"Are you okay to drive?" I asked.

"Yes, I only had the one beer and we were in there for over an hour."

"Okay." My phone beeped twice letting me know a text had arrived. I looked at my screen and read the text. "Betts and Sid are going to meet us back at the B & B."

"I like those kids," Olivia said.

"We'll try to figure this out later," Donovan said. "I'll even drive you back to the police station and the lake, tomorrow. You didn't see anyone in the boathouse, so I am sure everything is fine. The rest of the night we're all just going to relax. I'll get the fireplace going while you ladies pour us wine."

"How can I relax when the police suspect

me of murder, *two* murders?" I held up two fingers. "I have to find out who really killed Mrs. Brandon and Mindy and who set me up."

"We should do that," Olivia said. "We should figure it out over another glass of wine at the B & B."

"I don't need any more wine," I said.

"It's either that or an over the counter sleep aid," Olivia said, "Your choice."

The wine sounded like more fun.

CHAPTER 18

I didn't remember what time it was when I fell asleep. All I remembered was laying my head down on my pillow and closing my eyes.

It wasn't the alarm that woke me up, but the sun shining on my face. Even with a full night's sleep, my head pulsed. A bottle of water, two small blue pills, and a note sat on the nightstand. I opened the folded piece of paper and immediately recognized Olivia's handwriting.

Went for a walk. Take the medicine and drink ALL of the water. Take a shower and get dressed. I'll be back in thirty. O-

I gulped down the room temperature water with the two pills that held the promise of relieving me of my headache. I thought back to last night. Not the Sheriff's office or getting chased down in the parking lot by a woman who reminded me of a headmistress, but of the wine running through my veins and sensation of Donovan's hands around my waist.

As much as I wanted to curl up under the covers and daydream about Donovan, I needed to check out the boathouse.

I washed the smell of yesterday out of my hair and put on a pair of black leggings and an oversized white knit sweater. I opened the window an inch to get a whiff of fresh air. The sound of the church bells ringing in the distance echoed across town. I couldn't believe it was already Sunday and I hadn't completed the final draft my article yet.

I could see my editor tapping her watch letting me know my deadline was close at hand. In the six months I had worked at *Travel in the USA* I had never missed a deadline, but I came close almost every time. I suppose I could write the article from prison, because that's where I will be if I don't figure out what happened to Mindy and Mrs. Bandon by today.

"Kate!" Olivia said, a bit out of breath, as she burst through the bedroom door. Her hair was pulled in a ponytail exposing red ears. "It is magnificent out there. We are definitely going to start walking again when we get home." She pulled off her windbreaker then pushed her shoes and socks off with her toes. "I'm going to shower and I'll meet you downstairs for breakfast." Olivia said as she closed the bathroom door.

"Hurry up; you only have about thirty minutes left until Cora cleans up," I yelled through the door and left to get something to eat.

I wasn't sure if Sid and Betts stayed the night at the B & B or went back to Sid's mom's house, but they were seated at the dining room table in the same chairs as the day before. Billy was absent, same as the day before. I tilted the pitcher of orange juice over my glass and leered at Peter. His shoulders were slightly curved and his jaw loosened. His face had a pleasant look, almost like he was smiling inside. I hadn't seen him this at ease since I arrived and I wondered if he met his daughter last night at the lake.

"Kate," Donovan said.

As my name came out of Donovan's mouth

the orange juice started to overflow and run down my fingers and onto the floor. I placed both cup and pitcher on the wood credenza and grabbed a stack of napkins to clean up the mess.

"Something on your mind, Kate?" Sid asked.

"No, yes, no," I said, not wanting to admit I was watching Peter.

"I would say that sounds more like a yes." Betts said.

Donovan knelt beside me with a fresh stack of napkins and began wiping the sticky residue off the floor. "What's up, Kate?" His blue eyes were mere inches from mine.

"Nothing, I'm fine, thanks," I said.

I crumpled up the wad of sopping orange stained napkins and threw them in the waste basket. I grabbed a plate and piled it with turkey sausage, blueberry pancakes, and a handful of strawberries then sat next to Donovan.

Muffled coughs from the other end of the table filled the dining room. Peter held a napkin to his mouth and pushed out a few more coughs before quieting down. He nodded in our direction then went back to his eggs and grits.

Goose and Watson sauntered into the room, sat down next to the table leg and sniffed the floor where I had just spilled my drink. Watson looked up and scolded me with several quick chirps.

"I cleaned it up," I said to the Maine Coon.

Goose let out a loud "meow" and tapped my leg with his paw. He lifted his head and sniffed the fragrance of mouthwatering food that lingered in the air. I dipped my fingers in my syrup and bent down to let them lick off the sweet taste. Watson took a couple of sniffs then turned his head and walked away. He stopped in the doorway and furiously cleaned the fur closest to where my hand had been. Goose licked the sticky substance off until the tips of my fingers were completely clean. He strolled away with his tail swishing in the air. He stopped in the foyer and followed Watson's lead, cleaning his paws and the tuft of hair below his neck.

I glanced over at Peter. He was stacking his silverware and napkin on his plate. If I wanted to talk to him, I had to move fast.

"Peter, how are you enjoying the fall festival?"

His brow furrowed and he looked confused by the question. "I haven't really had a chance to go down there, but I plan on going today." He looked back down at his plate.

"Really, because I thought I saw you there yesterday coming out of the flower shop and in the book store." Everyone's eyes bounced back and forth between me and Peter as if they were watching a tennis match and it was the game point.

"Yes, I was just passing through."

I held my pancakes in place with my fork and cut a square small enough to bite. "How do you know Susan?"

"Susan?" Peter asked dumbfounded.

"Yes," I said. "She works at the bookstore. I saw you two talking."

"I was asking about a book." Peter looked at Donovan, Betts, and Sid, then back at me. "Is this what you wanted to talk to me about last night?"

"No." I shook my head. "But now that you mention it, if you have a few minutes, right now would be a good time to talk."

"I'm afraid I have somewhere to be." Peter picked up his plate and put it in the bin designated for dirty dishes.

He was in the foyer when I yelled out his name. He kept walking. I yelled louder, "Peter, you should check out the lake, it's quite stunning!" He shut the front door.

Olivia stood at the bottom of the stairs. She had put on a pair of jeans and a white, long sleeve shirt, topped off with a brown crochet cowl. "What was that all about?"

"I tried to talk to Peter, something I seem to keep failing to accomplish," I said.

Olivia filled her plate with fruit and a croissant and sat across the table next to Sid and Betts. "You really think he's the one who killed them?" Olivia asked.

"Yes," I said. "I think it's possible. Maybe he's here to do more than meet his daughter and Mindy and Mrs. Brandon found out, so he killed them. Maybe it had something to do with the papers we found in Billy's room."

"Billy was the last one to see his mom alive, that's something, right?" Olivia said. "His hefty inheritance gives him a motive to kill her."

"He's a momma's boy," Sid said. "I don't think he's going to know how to live without her. I don't think he has it in him to kill anyone."

"I need to go back to the Sheriff's station," I said. "I need to push him to take a good look at Peter."

A symphony of female voices echoed from the hall, almost competing to talk over one another.

As soon as they arrived in the foyer they grew quiet. Two familiar faces, Fanny and Ms. Belle, stood beside Cora in the doorway. It was clear they were here for a reason.

Cora interlaced her fingers and took a deep breath. "I've been talking to my friends and they tell me the four of you have been asking questions about me and my family." I opened my mouth to give an explanation, but knew not to speak when Cora shook her head at me. "My family is my business. If you want to know something you come and ask me. You don't go around starting rumors."

"What rumors? We didn't gossip," Betts said.

"The fact that you're asking questions in the first place makes people start talking, honey," Fanny said.

"Cora," I said. She raised her hand to shush me. I didn't stay quiet this time. "It is my job to ask questions. I have an article to write and if you want me to include this bed and breakfast and your name then I need to know some background on you and your family. Like, wouldn't it be interesting for the potential guests to know that the bed and breakfast has been in the same family for over a century and they can see the portraits of the original owners as they walk up the stairs to their room. Little tidbits like that give potential guests something to look forward to when they get here. It provides a little excitement. I need details if I am going to write an accurate article. Considering everything you've been through the past couple of days I didn't think it would be appropriate to ask you questions. It's not like I am prying into things like your finances." I looked at each one of the ladies faces to see if they were going to swallow what I was feeding them.

"Fine," Cora said. "What about the questions about Mindy? Why do you need to know about her?"

"Cora, I was arrested for suspicion of murder of Mrs. Brandon and the disappearance of Mindy, neither of which I participated in. So, yes, I am going to ask questions because I refuse to go to jail for something I didn't do."

"Well, you should have come to me," Cora said.

"And upset you more than you already are? No, I don't think so," I said.

The ladies looked at one another then back at us. Cora said, "What are your plans now?"

I wasn't sure if I should tell her about the lake. I didn't want her to think we were looking for Mindy's body out there. "I'm going to talk to Sheriff Gathers again. I found some more clues that could lead to Mrs. Brandon's killer and I want to make sure he's following up on them."

Cora's eyes widened. "What did you find?"

"Nothing you need to worry about."

"Then we're not going to go back to the lake?" Sid said.

I cringed.

"Why are you going out to the lake?" Cora asked. "Did you find something out there?"

"No, Cora, we just had a drink at the clubhouse last night and thought it would be nice to go back out there during the day. Maybe rent a boat and check out the lake itself."

"That was one of Mindy's favorite places to

go," Cora said. Fanny put her arm around Cora's shoulder.

"If we find out anything at all, Cora," I said, "I will let you know immediately."

"Thank you. Be careful at the lake," Cora said.

"What do we need to be careful of?" I asked.

"Snakes, spiders, things like that. And make sure you wear a life vest, you don't want to drown..." Cora's voice cracked.

"Come on, honey," Fanny said. "Let's go get you some coffee."

After breakfast we drove to the police station. The same scowl-faced woman that was at the front desk the night before stood in front of us.

"I need to see Sheriff Gathers," I said. "Please, it's very important."

"Sure," the puffy face woman said. "I'll get right on that." She kept her eyes locked on mine as she picked up a doughnut and took a bite. A chunk of the pastry fell from the bottom of her lip onto a stack of papers on the desk. She swiped it off and walked away.

I watched her saunter to the water color and pull a cone shaped paper cup from the silver cylinder. She drank the water in one swallow and then filled the cup again and repeated the process. When she was done she crumpled up the cup and threw it in the trash can then let out a loud, short burp.

"Ma'am," Olivia said to the defiant woman.

"Yeah, yeah, I'm getting' him," she said, and disappeared down the corridor.

I turned around and leaned against the counter with my back to the officer's desks. "She's not going to go get him," I said.

"We'll just wait until she does," Olivia said. "Why didn't Sid and his wife come with us?"

"His mom's car broke down and he's giving her a ride to meet her friends or something like that," I said. "He said they would meet us out at the lake when they're done."

"Kate." Donovan nodded in the direction behind me.

Dark, crescent shaped shadows lurked under the Sheriff's eyes and a day's worth of stubble had grown on his face. Even looking haggard, he was still intimidating. He weaved around the office desks and stopped at the reception counter.

"What can I do for you, Mrs. Westbrook?" He raised his eyebrows, "and friends?"

"Did you get a chance to look at any of the evidence I brought you yesterday?" I asked.

"Yes, we looked into it."

I waited for more information. When he didn't readily offer any I continued to question him. "Did you run tests on the flower petal?"

"It's being processed now," the Sheriff said.

"What about the shovel? Did you go to Peter's room and find it?"

"Yes, I had one of my deputies go out to Cora's and search Peter's room. We found it and brought it in."

I lifted my arms above my head like my favorite football team had just scored a touchdown then quickly lowered them. "So Peter's the main suspect now, I'm off the hook?"

"No, Mrs. Westbrook, not completely. There's still the matter of Mrs. Brandon. I'm not saying with certainty you were involved, but I'm not saying you weren't either. I need a little more time and I need you to stay in town a little longer."

"How can I convince you of my innocence?" I said. "What can I do to prove to you I didn't murder Mrs. Brandon?"

"What about the boathouse," Olivia said.

"What about it?" Donovan said.

"What boathouse?" Sheriff Gathers asked.

"We went to Lakeside Golf Club last night after we left here," Olivia said. "We were having a glass of wine in the lounge and we saw someone that looked exactly like the man Kate said she saw the day Mindy was killed. There were oleanders inside the boathouse the man came out of and there was a blanket and rope too. This was around seven forty five, just like what was written on the note we found in Billy's bedside drawer. A coincidence, I think not."

"You were drinking when you saw all of this?" Sheriff Gathers said.

"It was just a couple glasses of wine," Donovan said. "Not enough to obstruct one's judgment."

"What do you want me to do? There's no law saying you can't be at the lake at night. Listen," the Sheriff said, adjusting his belt, "I have work to do and I need you to let me do it and stop bugging me about every piece of paper you find and flower that has a blemish on it!" The Sheriff grumbled and stomped back down the hall.

The receptionist reclaimed her position at the desk and let out a mix between a grunt and a laugh. She wiped a few remaining crumbs off the stack of papers and lifted her eyes to mine. "You can go now."

CHAPTER 19

My phone chimed alerting me of a text message as Donovan, Olivia, and I pulled into the parking lot at Lakeside Golf Club. "Betts and Sid are here. They're parked behind the picnic table."

Donovan pulled into the space next to Sid's compact car. I rolled down my window and yelled out to Sid and Betts. "Hop in." Olivia scooted over and made room for the couple.

"It is freezing out there," Betts said, rubbing her hands together.

"So, what's the plan?" Sid asked.

"We need to get into that boathouse," I said.

"I don't think anyone's here. We're the only cars in the lot and I haven't seen anyone go in or come out of the clubhouse," Sid said.

"How long have you been here?" Olivia asked.

"Just a few minutes," Betts said.

"Listen," Sid said. "Last night I was thinking . . ."

"Here we go," Betts said, rolling her eyes.

"Oh, how I do love the way you think, Sid," I said, winking at Betts. "I would love to hear your theory, a little later."

"What if I'm right and it's too late."

"Point taken, please continue," I said.

Before Sid could get a word out, I spotted a man in a green jacket and baseball cap walk around the far corner of the clubhouse and start down the hill with what looked to be a heavy military bag slung over his shoulder.

"Sid, you're going to have to wait to tell us your theory. Look," I said, pointing across the field.

It wasn't until he reached the boathouse and turned his back to us that we saw the bag he was carrying had two arms and a head full of long blonde hair hanging out of it.

"No one panic," Donovan said. "Kate, call the police, Sid you and I..."

Two women ran up behind the man, coming from the same direction. The shorter of the two had long, straight brown hair that hung in her face. The taller woman was dressed in head to toe white, a shade brighter than her hair. Both women wore oversized round sunglasses that covered half of their face.

The man propped the limp girl on the ground against the building and reached up to remove the lock. The brunette held the door open allowing plenty of room for the white haired lady and the man to drag the unconscious, or dead, girl into the boathouse. Once everyone was inside the brunette slammed the door shut.

"What just happened?" Sid said.

"We need to call the police," Betts said. "We need to call them right now."

"Wait," I said.

"Wait? Are you kidding? They could be cutting that girl up right now, while we sit here," Betts said.

"That was Mindy," I said.

"Are you sure?" Olivia said.

"Yes."

"Then we most definitely need to call the police," Betts said. She pulled out her phone and dialed 9-1-1.

"That's a good idea, Betts," I said. "You stay here and keep the police on the phone. I'm going out there."

"We should wait for the cops, Kate," Donovan said.

"What if Betts is right?" Betts began to give the operator a detailed description of what we had just witnessed. I continued to plead my case. "I'm just going to knock on the door and see what happens."

"What if you become their next victim?" Olivia said.

"I'll be careful." I opened the door and got out before there were any more objections. Olivia and Donovan jogged to catch up with me as I bustled through the parking lot.

"Is Sid coming?" I asked.

"No, he's going to stay with Betts to make sure she stays calm and so nothing happens to her," Olivia said.

"We don't have much time before the police get here," I said.

"That's a good thing, right?" Olivia said.

I didn't answer. We were too close to the boathouse and I didn't want them to hear us talking. We slowed our pace and went around the side of the building. Strained voices bounced off the walls of the semi-bottomless structure. I put my ear to the cold wall, but I couldn't make out what they were saying.

Donovan stepped around the corner and reached up to knock on the door. I grabbed his forearm with my hand to stop him. I pointed to the window I had looked through the night before and whispered, "Help me up there so I can see inside. Olivia, stay on this side of the building and let us know if anyone comes out."

Olivia stood guard at the corner of the boathouse while Donovan and I climbed up the storage unit. I put all thoughts of Donovan out of my head and concentrated on each careful step.

We made it to the top of the storage container without incident. I motioned for Donovan to lift me up so I could see inside. He knelt down and I got on his shoulders. I poked my head over the sill and saw Mindy's body curled up in the corner next to the oleanders. I pulled out my cell phone and angled it to take a photo through the window. I was about to press the screen to take a picture when the man who was carrying Mindy's body came into view. It was Billy.

Donovan wobbled a little and I knew he would need to put me down soon. I positioned my phone so Billy and Mindy were both in the shot and tapped the screen at the exact moment the brunette walked into view. The phone clicked and a flash of light lit up the inside of the boathouse.

Their eyes shot up at the window and locked on mine. In the time it took me to register what had just happened, the trio was at the door.

"Run, Olivia, they're coming," I yelled and slid off Donovan's shoulders. We both jumped to the ground and headed to the edge of the water where Olivia was already running. The door to the boathouse slammed against the wall and reverberated over the lake.

"Stop or I'll shoot," one of the women yelled. "I'm not kidding."

The three of us stopped and stood facing the water. I could hear the woman moving through the grass, each step bringing her closer to us.

"Drop your phones on the ground and turn around."

"Please don't shoot us, I have a son and..." Olivia pleaded.

"I won't let anything happen to you," I said under my breath.

"Then don't make me," she said.

We turned around and were face to face with the woman with long brown hair, pointing a gun at us. "You're smarter than I gave you credit for," the woman said. She pulled off her sunglasses and dropped them to the ground. Her eyes were fierce and familiar. She took off her wig, revealing her bobbed blonde hair.

"Cora?" I said, momentarily shocked. "You killed your daughter?"

"I was wrong, you aren't that smart. I didn't *kill* my daughter."

Billy and the other woman joined Cora. "You took off your wig," the woman said.

"No point in keeping them on now that they're right here in front of us."

The taller woman's white wig and sunglasses came off exposing Ms. Belle's face.

I glanced up at the clubhouse, at the wall of dark windows. I looked to the front door hoping the lady with the tight bun was watching.

"They're not open yet," Billy said. "They won't open for another twenty minutes."

"Did you kill your mom?" Donovan asked.

"No, I did not. I am not part of this sick plan." Billy flipped his hand at the two women.

"Shut up, Billy," Cora said.

"They said I had to come here or they would kill me next. I don't plan on dying anytime soon. I will do whatever I have to, to stay alive, even if that means you three have to die."

"Billy," Ms. Belle said. "Let's you and me take a walk by the lake." She tucked her arm in his and led him to the water.

"Why?" I said to Cora.

"Why? You really have to ask why? You should know you're the one prying in my business. Why don't you tell me why I killed Mrs. Brandon, or should I say, mother."

"Money," I said.

"It always comes down to money, doesn't it? You know she had the nerve to tell me she wasn't going to leave me anything in her will. She said the only reason she was telling me she was my mom was because my father was in town for the first time in decades and she wanted to get him back for marrying her best friend. Can you believe that?"

"I'm sorry, Cora, but you didn't have to kill her," I said.

"Yes, I did. For over twenty years I have taken orders from that tyrant. All those years I had to struggle just to put food on the table and that old woman would come into town and want me to kiss her diamond filled fingers. Never once did she help me. She would tell me how lucky I was to have an employer like her - an employer. I bowed down to her every order because I loved that B & B. It was my home." Cora shifted her weight and raised the gun a few inches. "She knew for months I was looking for my birth mother and she never once said a word, not until she found out my father would be here. When she finally did tell me who she really was, she said after this weekend I needed to pack my bags and leave because her son, Billy, was going to be taking over the bed and breakfast. I wasn't about to let her kick me out of my home and I am not about to let Billy either. Now move it," Cora said, pointing us to the boathouse.

I walked in front of Olivia while Donovan stayed behind her. Cora kept her distance and the gun aimed at us until we reached the entrance.

The floor was shaped like a horseshoe. The section below the boat was cut out to allow it to be lowered into the water. Mindy lay in the far corner on top of the bag she was stuffed in when she was carried into the building. The bouquet of oleanders sat next to her outstretched arm. Mindy's eyes were closed and her skin was pale. A small dark spot in her hair, next to her scalp, looked like it could be dried blood. I leaned back and focused on her torso. I could see her chest rise and fall. I was relieved she was still alive.

"Cora, think about what you're doing," Donovan said.

"I have thought about it, for days. Mother was clean and easy, nothing a little oleander in her tea couldn't fix. It worked great on my husband. That's how I knew it would take care of that old bat too. And as soon as Billy gives me the locket, I'll get rid of him with a little bullet to the brain. It'll be a little messier, but just as effective. I suppose I will need to get rid of you three the same way. That's actually not a bad idea. It'll look like there's a serial killer on the loose. I'm getting better and better at this."

I didn't want to die. I wasn't ready to die. The only thing I could think to do was keep her talking while I tried figure a way out of this situation before it got even more out of hand. "You said something about the locket," I said.

"Mrs. Brandon, *mother*, was wearing it when she arrived. She said it fell off her neck when she was outside, but I have looked everywhere and I can't find it which means Billy has it."

"What's so important about the locket?" Olivia said.

We stood side by side next to the water, the boat hanging above our heads. Cora pushed a button on the wall and the boat began to lower.

"The combination to her house safe is etched on the inside." Cora let out a heavy sigh. "Look at what you've done, Kate. You should have just taken the murder rap and lived out your days in prison. Now I'm going to have to kill all three of you. Their deaths are on you."

"Before you do," I said, "what happened to Mindy? Did you make her drink oleander tea too?" I motioned to her slumped body.

"No, but we have had to keep her sedated. She's a bit feisty. Belle's brother helped out with her, for a small cut of my inheritance. I told Mindy to go pick some white roses to put in your room. Belle's brother was behind the greenhouse and he was supposed to daze her then bring her here. I was going to set it up so it looked like you had done something to her. You saved me the trouble by seeing it happen then running around saying she was murdered."

The boat finished its decent into the dark water.

"Why did you involve Mindy?" Olivia asked. "She's your daughter. You could have really hurt her."

"We wouldn't have had to if she had just kept her mouth shut about our plan, but she went around asking people if they had heard the rumor about us being heirs to the Harmond family fortune. She told people we were going to be rich when the old lady died. We had already planned on framing you for Mrs. Brandon's murder," Cora said, nodding in my direction. "But Belle came up an idea of how to shut Mindy up and make you look even guiltier."

"Was Belle's brother the one who put the shovel in Peter's room?" I said.

Cora let out a quick burst of laughter. "Talk about luck, I had no idea Peter was going to be in that room. We put it in there just to get it out of the way, but what a great way to pin Mindy's disappearance on him, if the charge didn't stick with you, of course. Now stop asking questions and get in the boat."

The motor boat swayed and as we stepped inside. We each sat on one of the small cushioned seats. I looked at Olivia then to Donovan. Olivia's worried eyes ran over the boat and then Cora's hand, holding the gun. I could tell by the wrinkle between Donovan's eyebrows he was deep in thought; I imagined he was thinking about how to get us out of this situation.

Cora hit the wall of the boathouse with the butt of the gun twice. A minute later Billy and Ms. Belle entered the room.

"Billy, unchain the boat from the lift and get

in, you're driving. Belle, stay here in case Mindy wakes up," Cora said. She waited for Billy to unhook the boat and then hopped in after him. She sat in the passenger seat, in front of me.

"Why did you set me up?" I said.

"What better way to get publicity. I can see the headline: Travel Writer Commits Murder While on Assignment. It's Brilliant."

"How did Mrs. Brandon get my scarf around her neck?" I said.

"You ask too many questions!" Cora said.

"I have a right to know."

"I thought you were with lover boy there," Cora said, annoyed as she waved the gun in Donovan's direction. "I tried to get in your room, but the door was locked and I had forgotten to bring my master key with me. I was about to run upstairs and get it when I saw your shadow. I decided to wait until breakfast the next morning and go in and get it. I knew Mrs. Brandon was already dead, so it was real easy to run in her room and put it around her neck before coming downstairs."

Cora lowered the gun to her thigh as the boat crept out of its docked spot. "Don't look so scared, Kate. I'll make it quick and painless." Cora said.

Olivia's head sagged as she focused on the floor of the boat. I knew she was thinking about Leo. My heart was heavy at the thought of Leo losing his mother and me losing my best friend. I promised I would keep her safe and I would do everything I could to keep that promise. How I was going to do that, I didn't know. How does one get away from a gun toting angry woman, on a boat, in the middle of the lake? I needed to think of something fast because we were almost to the wooded area across from the boat launch.

I looked over at the parking lot to see if flashing blue lights had made it yet. The only vehicles I saw were Sid's and Donovan's. I wondered if Sheriff Gathers had anything to do with Cora's scheme. I doubted it, but I did know of one unsavory cop, Ms. Belle's brother. I hoped he wasn't the one who got the call to come out here and check on the situation.

The boat jerked and sputtered to a stop.

"What's going on? Why did you stop?" Cora said to Billy.

"I didn't. See for yourself." Billy said, pointing to the round gauge with the red needle sitting on top of the letter E. "You didn't put gas in the boat."

"You think I'm some sort of idiot. Of course I put gas in the boat."

The distraction provided the perfect moment to make a move. I pushed Olivia overboard. The loud splash and spray of water into the boat startled Cora and Billy. Donovan lurched forward and wrapped a strong arm around Billy's neck and they began to wrestle.

I grabbed Cora's wrist and pushed her arm up in the air then slammed it down on the windshield. The gun flew out of her hand and teetered on the bow of the boat. Cora kicked my bruised thigh knocking me back against the seats. A pulsing pain shot through my leg taking my breath away. I gave myself a couple of seconds and then pulled myself up. I saw Cora fling her body over the glass and stretch her arm out, reaching for the gun. I snatched the collar of her shirt and pulled her back before she could lock her fingers around the pistol. The boat rocked hard and Donovan and Billy were tossed in the water where they continued to wrestle.

Cora twisted in my grip and body slammed me hard enough I landed on the rear end of the boat, inches from the water. I lifted up and was about to run at Cora when I heard the crack of gunfire echo off the lake. I grabbed the back of the seat to pull myself forward and my finger slid in the hole where the bullet had entered the cushion, next to my leg. I looked up and saw Cora aiming the gun at me.

"Cora, don't. Please."

"Beg all you want it's…" Olivia reached up and grabbed Cora's shirt pulling her into the lake.

I locked my arm around Olivia's and helped her into the boat. I scanned the water for Cora, but I couldn't see her. The boat began to wobble and I turned around expecting to see a sopping wet woman crawling back on board. Instead, I watched Donovan swing a leg over the edge of the boat. I grabbed his arm and helped pull him in.

"Where's Billy?" I said.

Donovan pointed to alternating splashes of water and a bobbing head swimming back to shore. "Where's Cora?" Donovan asked.

"I don't know where she is," Olivia said.

Olivia and I leaned over opposite sides of the boat in search of Cora. Donovan stood and looked over the bow.

"I don't see her, do you?" I asked.

A loud growl coming from the back of the boat grabbed our attention. Cora seethed as she climbed aboard. I didn't see the gun, but that didn't mean she didn't have it. I reared my arm back and punched her in the face hard enough to knock her on her side, stunned. My knuckles stung from the impact and I shook my hand out.

Donovan unwound the rope attached to the inside of the boat and tied Cora to the passenger seat before she came to her senses.

"Now what do we do?" Olivia said. "We're out of gas."

"I'm going to tell everyone you kidnapped me. Sheriff Gathers will believe me over you three any day," Cora said.

"Oh, good, she's fully awake," Olivia said with a hint of sarcasm.

Sirens and flashing lights from a small green and brown boat headed in our direction from the shore. While we waited for our rescue we watched three police officers enter the boathouse. A minute later one of the officers came out with Mindy who was still a bit unsteady. The EMT's raced to her side and began a routine check on her.

"Look." I pointed to the top of the stairs where the tight bun lady stood with her hands on her hips.

"Betts and Sid are waiting for us," Donovan said, motioning to the covered picnic table where the two were standing on top of the bench.

"You okay?" I asked Olivia.

"Yeah, how about you?"

"I'm good. I could use a drink though, and a blanket." We both leaned against the side of the boat and let our bodies relax.

"Listen, next time you decide to push me overboard, give me a little notice," Olivia said, smiling.

"Will do. It was good thinking though, right?"

Olivia nodded. "It was good thinking."

"I'm fine too, thanks for asking," Donovan said.

"We already know that." Olivia winked at Donovan.

Cora twisted and turned in her seat in an attempt to escape from the rope. She went on about how she was going to blame us for everything that had just transpired, but I blocked her out. My focus was on Donovan's soaked sweater and pants and how nicely they clung to his body. He was in great shape, better than I thought.

I didn't realize I was staring at him until Olivia cleared her throat. I pulled my eyes up and saw Donovan smile at me, and then turn to look at the police boat that pulled up beside us.

"Busted," Olivia said under her breath and chuckled.

The EMT's gave us blankets and checked our bodies for scrapes, cuts, bumps, and bruises. Cora was handcuffed and lowered into a squad car with Ms. Belle. Sheriff Gathers took off his hat and rubbed his face with his hand. For a moment I felt sympathy for him, but then I remembered he was more than likely having an affair with a married woman and the empathy vanished.

"This is a bit different than the last time we were on a boat on the lake," Olivia said.

"Not much, we still ended up in the water," I said.

By the time the police were finished taking

all of our statements it was three o'clock and my stomach was rumbling. I wanted a shower and the biggest plate of food I could find.

CHAPTER 20

I opened the door to my bathroom and let the steam from my hot shower escape the cramped space. No matter how small the bathroom was, I was grateful I didn't have to share one with the other guests.

Cora was so proud of this room and so full of energy when I arrived. Forty – eight hours later and she's in jail for murder, attempted murder, and kidnapping. How could so much change in such a small period of time?

"You ready?" Olivia said.

I walked out of the bathroom and tucked my blue button up shirt into my jeans. The chill had finally left my bones and the smell of the lake in my hair was replaced with the aroma of my mint conditioner. "Now I'm ready," I said.

"You sure you're all right?"

"Yeah, I'm just tired and relieved. I'm glad this is all over. How about you?"

"Better. I was scared when Cora had the gun on us. All I could think about was Leo. I couldn't imagine him growing up without a mom. I couldn't imagine not seeing him grow up. I didn't want anything to happen to you either, so no more of this almost getting us killed stuff."

"I think once in a lifetime is enough for me."

"Don't forget we start our workouts in the

morning. You need an accountability partner." Olivia said. "By the way, we're doing three miles a day, so be ready."

"I can't go walking tomorrow. I have to write my article," I said.

"Okay, then Tuesday. No excuses. Tonight we're going to eat, drink…"

"No more wine," I said.

"…drink whatever, and be merry."

"Done and done. Let's go," I said.

Olivia paused before opening the bedroom door. "So, what's going on with you and Donovan?"

"I don't know. It's like we get this close to kissing," I held my thumb and pointer finger an inch apart, "and then something happens and the moment's over. Maybe he doesn't know I'm interested in him."

"Oh, he knows," Olivia said as she opened the door.

"Probably," I said, shrugging. I waited until the door was closed then twisted the knob to make sure it was locked. We were about to head downstairs when the red door leading to the third floor apartment opened and Mindy step out with slumped shoulders and tangled hair.

What do you say to the daughter of the woman who tried to kill you? Sorry your mom's in jail? I didn't want to lie. Maybe a nod of recognition would be enough. Apparently she didn't know what to do either because she froze in place and stared us.

Olivia broke the uncomfortable silence. "What will you do now, with the Bed and Breakfast?"

Mindy lifted her shoulders and pushed a clump of hair away from her face. "I don't want this place. I hate living here. Mrs. Brandon's son can have it, for a price," Mindy said and hustled down the flight of steps before we had a chance to reply.

"Okay, that was interesting," Olivia said.

"She is definitely her mother's daughter."

Watson and Goose were the only ones in the foyer when we reached the bottom of the stairs. I leaned over and rubbed the top of Goose's head with the tips of my fingers. "What's going to happen to you two now?"

"They'll stay with me," Billy said. "It's time for social hour. I don't have any food prepared, but there's plenty of alcohol." Billy held up a short glass filled to the rim with a gold liquid.

"That's okay, Billy, we're going to head downtown," I said. I felt sorry for him. He had gained and lost so much in just a matter of a few days. What was he going to do now? How would he cope? My thoughts didn't stay on Billy long. I was distracted by the fresh dose of Polo coming from the staircase.

Olivia looked at me then turned her attention to Donovan. "Someone smells good tonight."

"Thank you," Donovan said. "Are you ladies ready to go?"

"Sure," I said. "Have you heard from Betts and Sid?"

"They're at Sid's mom's house trying to convince her they're okay," Donovan said. "Where are we going to eat?"

The front door opened and Peter walked in with a radiant smile. I knew why as soon as I saw the young girl in an oversized Atlanta Falcons sweatshirt and ripped jeans walk in behind him.

"Everyone, I would like you to meet my daughter, Sarah." Sarah greeted us with a small voice and lifted her hand in a quick wave.

Peter looked at his daughter and said, "Why don't you put your bag in my room and then we'll head downtown. It's down this hall; make a right when you get in the kitchen, past the refrigerator." Peter watched Sarah until she was out of sight then turned to me. "Listen, Kate, I want to apologize for the way I've been acting the past two days. This was my only shot at getting to see my daughter, who I haven't seen in years, and I needed to stay focused on her. Her mom took her and moved away and didn't tell me where they were. It took two years to track her down. Anyway, you said you wanted to talk to me about something, earlier?"

"Why were you in the backyard the day Mindy disappeared?"

Peter nodded. "I was looking for anything that could help me figure out where Mindy was taken. When I was looking for Sarah I met Cora and Mindy. When I was describing her Mindy said she knew her. Sarah's in high school, but takes a college course for extra credit and they have a class together. Mindy said she could help me get in touch with her. She was the middle man, at least until a few weeks ago. Something must have happened with her because Mindy said she couldn't help me anymore, but a lady name Susan could."

"Susan, from the bookstore," I said.

"Yes, that's her."

Sarah came down the hall with her hands in her pants pocket. "I put my stuff up. Where am I going to sleep?"

"You can have the bed," Peter said. "I'll take the floor."

"No you won't," Billy said. "You can have the room my mother and I were staying in. There are two beds in there, and a bathroom." Billy took two swallows of his drink and retreated to the living room.

"Dad, we should get going. The festival ends early tonight," Sarah said.

"Dad," Peter said. "I didn't know if I would ever hear you call me that again."

"Come on, dad." Sarah rolled her eyes and tried to hold back a smile.

Peter opened the front door and was met by Betts and Sid. He moved aside and let them through then left with his daughter.

"Who was that with Peter?" Betts asked.

"That couldn't have been Peter, that guy was happy," Sid said.

"He found his daughter," Olivia said.

"I'm so glad," Betts said.

"Have you guys turned on the TV?" Sid asked. "Cora and Ms. Belle are all over the news. Camera crews are down at the lake. They didn't mention any of us by name. They're referring to us as the guests at Harmony Bed & Breakfast."

"I'll read about it tomorrow," I said. "We're headed to dinner downtown then the festival. You want to come with us?"

Sid opened the front door and stepped back, "ladies first."

None of us was in the mood to walk. We agreed to let Donovan drive us the few blocks to the festivities. The crowd had thinned out and the police had opened up the lane they had previously blocked to allow the overflow of patrons. The sun had almost set and shop lights had begun to illuminate the sidewalks. Donovan pulled into a parking space in front of In Bloom Florist.

I had a fondness for Stewart the moment I met him and I wanted to stop in and say goodbye. A small bistro on the same block, but at the opposite end of Stewart's shop, had started to form a line. I told my crew to go ahead of me and I would catch up.

The fragrance of fall filled the little store and I knew every time I smelled that combination of aromas I would think of Stewart. I followed the sound of Stewart's hearty laughter and found him behind the counter showing another gentleman the original brick floor.

"Mr. Williams, what a wonderful surprise to see you," I said, offering my hand.

"Kate, it's good to see you too, and in one piece. I heard what happened at the lake. I am so sorry you and your friends had to go through all of that."

"I'm okay, but I am concerned about you. How are you holding up?"

"I'm just trying to take it all in."

"You two know each other," Stewart said.

"Yes, I met her down at Lakeside Golf Club when I was feeding the birds," Mr. Williams said.

"Kate," Stewart said. "Do you know that we have been friends since grade school? I didn't know if I'd ever see my old buddy again." Stewart slapped Mr. Williams back a couple of times. "It's so good to see him again."

They looked like they hadn't spent a day apart.

"Stewart, I wanted to stop in and say goodbye. I'll be leaving tonight or in the morning," I said.

"My sweet Kate," Stewart said, pressing his lips lightly on the top of my hand. "It has been a pleasure meeting you."

"And it has been a pleasure meeting you." I gave a little bow. "I'll send you a copy of next month's *Travel in the USA*."

"How wonderful!" Stewart seemed genuinely excited.

"I have to go. It was good seeing you both. Maybe I'll see you again next fall." I left the shop slightly better for having met those two men.

Dinner was relaxed and filled with laughter. After we finished eating we walked through the park, stopping off at Fanny's table to say goodbye. She told us she didn't think we had anything to do with Mindy, but as a friend she had to support Cora no matter what she thought. I appreciated her loyalty even if I didn't agree with her.

The night was what I had imagined the entire weekend would have felt like if Cora and Ms. Belle hadn't kidnapped Mindy and killed Mrs. Brandon and tried to pin it on me.

After a pleasant evening we headed back to the Bed and Breakfast. Olivia went upstairs and grabbed her bag then joined me, Donovan, Betts, and Sid in the foyer to say farewell.

"Do you have to leave tonight?" I said.

"I have class in the morning," Olivia said.

"Call in sick. They'll get a sub to cover you."

Olivia tilted her head down and her eyes up giving me one of her many motherly looks she had formed over the years. "I'll come by your house tomorrow night. Bye everyone," Olivia said, waving as she walked out.

I stood on the porch to make sure she got to her van okay. "Call me when you get home so I know you made it," I yelled out.

"Kate," Betts said. "We would stay another night, but I just don't think I can. We're going to head back home. It's been great getting to know you. I don't think I could have gotten through this weekend without you and Donovan."

"Hey now," Sid said.

"You know what I mean. Seriously though, thanks for including us and all."

I wrapped my arms around Betts. "I need to be the one thanking you guys. I couldn't have cleared my name without all of your help, all three of you."

"Sid." Donovan grabbed his hand and shook it. "Take care of that sweet wife of yours." Donovan turned to Betts. "And good luck with him," he said and winked at her.

Betts and Sid walked to their car leaving me and Donovan alone on the porch. Another great moment for a kiss, but I wasn't counting on it. Besides, I was shivering and wanted to go inside.

The crackle of wood burning in the fireplace gave off ample heat and I warmed quickly. "I wonder where Billy is," I said.

"Maybe he went to pass out somewhere," Donovan said. "Want to sit down?"

We shared the couch and let the heat from the fire warm us. Our bodies weren't touching, but I could feel the magnetism of his leg next to mine. My heart fluttered. He leaned forward and rested his

227

elbows on his knees, lacing his fingers.

I couldn't stand the silence. "And then there were four," I said.

He turned to me. "Four?"

"Me, you, Watson, and Goose," I said, pointing to the window where half of Watson's body was covered by the curtain. He was spying on us, I was sure. Goose laid on his back, legs sprawled in the air, next to the hearth.

Donovan leaned back against the couch. His eyes locked on mine. I wanted to look away, but I couldn't. This was another perfect moment for a kiss. Would we miss this opportunity like all the others?

I expected him to look away or get up. Instead, he wrapped his hand around the side of my face pulling me close to him and pressed his lips against mine. He was worth the wait.

There is a misconception about Florida; it never gets cold. This is not true for the panhandle, at least not in recent years. This past decade we experienced snow flurries, an ice storm, and several nights of below freezing temperatures. The temperature tonight reached the low forties, and the wind chill made it even colder.

But none of that mattered. All I wanted to do was curl up in my rocker on my front porch and let the memories of Donovan and last night keep me warm.

Olivia pulled her van into my driveway and raced to the porch to get out of the wind. "What in the world are you doing sitting outside in the cold?"

I wrapped my down blanket tighter around me and took a sip of my hot cocoa. "There's a blanket inside the door for you and a cup of hot chocolate on the table. Bring it out here and sit with me. Bring the manila folder that's on the table too."

Olivia curled up in her blanket and sat in the chair next to mine. "Why aren't you inside where it's warm and, wait a minute, I know that look. I want to know everything. I want details."

I told her about the first kiss and the subsequent kisses that took place throughout the evening. "We stayed up all night talking. We're going to meet in Atlanta next month."

"Will you be staying in Harmonyville?" Olivia said.

"No, I'll be staying downtown in a name brand hotel, thank you very much. I think Harmonyville, Georgia, is delightful and lovely and all, but I've had my share of that place for a while."

I pulled the single space, typed page out of the manila folder and handed it to Olivia.

Festivities and Fun in Harmonyville, Georgia

Located an hour south of Atlanta, the small town of Harmonyville, Georgia, is filled with historic charm, family fun, and tradition. This October was no exception as the town celebrated the tenth anniversary of its fall festival...

"Well done," Olivia said. "So, what's next?"

"Some traditional holiday events over the next few months and then in March we're headed to Louisiana."

"*We* are?" Olivia said.

"Yes, you're coming with me."

"To new adventures," Olivia said. She held up her mug of hot chocolate. We clanked our cups together.

"To new adventures."

ABOUT THE AUTHOR

Rebecca Pappas is not only an author but an artist as well. When she isn't writing, drawing or painting, she loves to go to the beach, crochet, craft, take long walks, and spend time with her family and friends. She lives in Florida with her two cats, Bogie and Bryce.

CPSIA information can be obtained at www.ICGtesting.com
Printed in the USA
LVOW06s2127301215

468538LV00001B/7/P